"Birdie, I don't have to listen to this." Timmy turned away and Birdie reached out to clutch his arm.

"Just listen, Timmy! 'I had to see everything . . . the whole grisly, interminable business.' "

Timmy shook himself free. "Birdie! For God's sake, why are you doing this?"

But her voice rolled on strangely in a kind of hypnotic horror about mass graves and hair-cutting and chimneys. She paused a moment and this time Timmy did not interrupt. She reached out quietly and took his hand. He pressed it hard into a fist while she held it lightly. "And then, Timmy, he says, 'I had to look through the peephole.' Peephole," she repeated. Her voice grew small as if in wonder over the very sound of the word. " 'I had to look through the peephole of the gas chamber and watch the process of death itself.' "

For one horrible moment it was as if they felt themselves, both sister and brother, looking through the peephole of death. "Hoess said," Birdie continued, "that in order to do this he had to 'exercise intense self-control . . . in order to prevent my innermost doubts . . . I was forced to bury all human considerations as deeply as possible.' " Birdie stopped. She was still holding his hand.

"Timmy, I know you didn't kill, but how deeply did you have to bury your innermost doubts and feelings while you watched this 'prank'?"

Timmy looked directly at her, the communion between them unbroken. His skin was blotchy and red, but his eyes were like dark voids. "Birdie," he whispered, "it was real. I am the prank, and there is no place to bury anything in a prank."

KATHRYN LASKY is the author of several books including *Beyond the Divide* (available in a Laurel-Leaf edition). She lives in Cambridge, Massachusetts, with her husband and their two children.

ALSO AVAILABLE IN LAUREL-LEAF BOOKS:

QUANTITY SALES

Most Dell Books are available at special quantity discounts when purchased in bulk by corporations, organizations, and special-interest groups. Custom imprinting or excerpting can also be done to fit special needs. For details write: Dell Publishing Co., Inc., 1 Dag Hammarskjold Plaza, New York, NY 10017, Attn.: Special Sales Dept., or phone: (212) 605-3319.

INDIVIDUAL SALES

Are there any Dell Books you want but cannot find in your local stores? If so, you can order them directly from us. You can get any Dell book in print. Simply include the book's title, author, and ISBN number, if you have it, along with a check or money order (no cash can be accepted) for the full retail price plus 75¢ per copy to cover shipping and handling. Mail to: Dell Readers Service, Dept. FM, P.O. Box 1000, Pine Brook, NJ 07058.

KATHRYN LASKY

LAUREL-LEAF
BOOKS

LAUREL-LEAF BOOKS bring together under a single imprint outstanding works of fiction and nonfiction particularly suitable for young adult readers, both in and out of the classroom. Charles F. Reasoner, Professor Emeritus of Children's Literature and Reading, New York University, is consultant to this series.

Published by
Dell Publishing Co., Inc.
1 Dag Hammarskjold Plaza
New York, New York 10017

Excerpts on pages 19 and 23 from the Apple Jacks jingle used with permission of Kellogg Company. © 1981 Kellogg Company.

Excerpt on page 80 from NIGHT by Elie Wiesel, translated by Stella Rodway. Copyright © Les Editions de Minuit 1958. English translation copyright © MacGibbon & Kee 1960. Reprinted by permission of Hill and Wang (a division of Farrar, Straus and Giroux, Inc.).

Excerpts on pages 89 and 98–99 from COMMANDANT OF AUSCHWITZ by Rudolph Hoess; published by Weidenfeld & Nicolson, London. © 1951 Wydawnictwo Prawnicze, Warsaw. English translation © 1959 by George Weidenfeld and Nicolson, London.

Laurel-Leaf Library ® TM 766734, Dell Publishing Co., Inc.

ISBN: 0-440-97144-6

RL: 6.0

Reprinted by arrangement with Macmillan Publishing Company

Printed in the United States of America

November 1986

10 9 8 7 6 5 4 3 2 1

WFH

CHAPTER

1

The bell rang, and students flooded out of classrooms into the wide corridors without the usual in-between-classes frenzy of movement. They took their time walking to their lockers, as it was nearly noon and lunch-hour socializing began in the hallways.

Birdie Flynn came out of English Composition. She was absorbed in reading Miss Edland's comments on her impressionistic mood piece on the Boston skyline at sunset. "Excellent" was Miss Edland's comment on the phrase: "All fiery and outlined by the low-angled November sun"; a few lines later, "mighty structures" was circled and "overwritten" was penciled in the margin. A hand pulled sharply at Birdie's elbow.

"There's no yogurt for lunch. The truck didn't get here. Want to go to Santarpio's and get a pizza?"

"If I were as skinny as you, I would," Birdie replied to her best friend, Gloria Saccharelli, who wore size four jeans and sometimes still had to take them in.

"There's not only no yogurt for lunch, there are no passes either," Michael O'Hare said. He was standing in between Gloria and another girl, Simone Dennis.

"Why not?" both Gloria and Birdie asked simultaneously.

"Because of what happened at the Chelsea Street synagogue."

"What happened?" Birdie asked.

"You don't know?" Michael replied, rather too pointedly.

"No, I don't. Should I?"

Michael snorted.

Simone spoke up. "Some kids went down there Friday night and messed the place up."

"So what's the big deal?" asked Gloria. She was still holding Birdie's elbow. "Why no passes? Why no pizza?"

"The cops are coming to sniff around," Michael answered. There were groans from everyone but Birdie. "Where've you been, Birdie, that you didn't hear about it?"

"I don't know. I was in English."

"And you take English Comp at that, with all the Jews— not Business English like us. Weren't they talking about it?"

"No. We were talking about color and light in writing."

"You mean colored and kikes!"

"You're gross," Birdie said.

"Come off it, Michael," Gloria snapped.

"Joke! Joke!" Michael raised his hand defensively.

2

"It's a joke," Simone said.

"Some joke," Birdie replied.

"Jews don't need Business English." Simone giggled and looked at Michael for support. "That's what my dad would say."

"Shhhhh!" Gloria warned. The group dropped their voices suddenly as three students walked by.

"They didn't hear us. Come on," Michael urged, "let's go get lunch."

They were almost the first ones in the lunchroom. Rank upon rank of gray Formica tables stretched across the space. The cinderblock walls had been left unpainted, which Birdie guessed was preferable to the pale green walls of the old part of the school. Behind the long counter, pale ladies with hairnets plunged ladles into vats of macaroni and tonged up hot dogs. In line, Birdie heard two other kids talking about the Chelsea Street synagogue. It seemed funny that she had missed hearing about it until now.

Birdie put her tray down on the table. She removed the bread from her bologna sandwich. She scraped the glob of whipped cream from the cube of Jell-O. Michael, who was sitting across from her, looked at her plate. "Do you ever eat anything *with*, Birdie?"

"What do you mean?"

"Look, you're having a bologna sandwich without bread, a salad without dressing, Jell-O without whipped cream and skim milk."

"Just watching my figure."

"You're not that fat."

"Thanks a bunch."

"Now, that is really gross, Michael," Simone said. "If you said that to me I'd really be pissed. You should apologize."

"Forget it," Birdie said. She was scanning the lunchroom. "Anybody seen my brother Timmy?"

"I think he might have cut."

"No, he didn't," Birdie said firmly. "I saw him after second period."

"Yeah, but he wasn't in Business English," Simone said.

"And Skeeter wasn't in Basic Math," Gloria added.

"And no sign of Mooch."

"Oh, no!" Birdie sighed.

Just at that moment, a hush fell over the lunchroom as two policemen appeared in the doorway with the principal. There was only the sound of cutlery and dishes and the dishwashing machines hissing from the kitchen area. The students continued to eat, their heads bent, their eyes fixed on the plastic plates. It was not the silence of fear, but of power. It was like a phalanx, and Birdie felt herself locked within it. Not a glance was stolen, not a word spoken, for that was how it worked—no movement, no voice. And it did work. The two policemen and the principal turned and left. The talking resumed almost instantly, and the inarticulate hum—the white noise of the lunchroom—swelled again.

The tables were breaking up now. Birdie made her way through the aisles toward the window between the kitchen and the lunchroom to leave her tray. She heard snatches of conver-

4

sation as she went—about the cops, about the synagogue. She didn't pay much attention. She wanted to go to the library, away from the school lunchroom with its din, or worse, its iron-clad silence. Either way it felt oppressive. The cool silence of the library was different, a place for thinking and dreaming and not worrying about getting fat or anything else.

Walking home from school, it was all uphill to the Flynn house on the point. To the right was the harbor and across the harbor, Boston. To the left was Birdie's neighborhood, East Boston, Maverick Square and then a tangle of ramps and overpasses that shot straight into Logan Airport. As Birdie walked she mostly looked right. It was a gray, overcast June day. The water appeared leaden and still. Even on a sunny day the water looked gray. Last semester Birdie had read the *Odyssey*. Homer kept talking about the "wine dark sea," and she couldn't help but wonder sometimes what he would have done if he had been born in East Boston. The harbor never looked wine dark. Usually it was gray and sometimes, on a winter day, when the wind whipped up the whitecaps, it was black, but wine dark—never. This shouldn't matter, according to Miss Edland. Miss Edland said that all life was a search for metaphor. Birdie was not really sure what she meant by that remark. Right now, on her way home, it was a search for Timmy, Birdie's older brother. She looked down the piers that reached out from Border Street. If Timmy was alone, there was a good chance that he might be on one of the piers. But if he was with Skeeter or Mooch, there was no telling where he would be.

There was a kind of haphazard rhythm to both sides of the streets, Birdie thought. Empty lots alternated with warehouses and burned-out buildings. They formed a dilapidated landscape punctuated by views of Boston across the water—the new Boston with its renovated wharf condominiums and hotels mixed in with steel and glass skyscrapers. Almost in the dead center of this skyline was the Customs House tower. Neither renovated nor new, it looked gray and funky to Birdie. She liked it. For some reason it always made her think of the house of the old lady who lived in a shoe from the book that the Head Start teacher had read to her nearly twelve years ago. She had been about four, but she still remembered the picture of that crazy shoe—all lopsided and funny looking but a cozy place to be. The tower was not lopsided at all, but there was something humorous about the way it stood there, improbable amidst the steel and the renovated brick and granite buildings.

There was nothing funky or humorous about this side of the harbor, the East Boston side. The brick of the new buildings didn't even try to look old. The oldest parts of East Boston had gradually been torn down, starting over thirty years ago when people were into urban renewal, not renovation. Finally they gave up on renewal and went in for airport extension. The runways were just a half mile away now. As she approached the local housing project, Birdie noticed that the fountain in the courtyard was not running, and graffiti could clearly be seen on the vertical stone columns from which the water had once sprayed.

There was still no sign of Timmy, and she had just passed

the last pier. This wasn't good. Timmy had been flirting with his last cut. If he took it now, even so close to the end of school, it meant he was out. He had probably flunked three out of four courses anyway, but to have disciplinary action in addition to academic failure meant that he would not even be able to go to summer school. If their dad found out—Birdie didn't want to think about that.

The fish truck was parked at the corner of Sumner and Orleans. Joe T. was selling from the back. Two nuns were buying haddock, and he was trying to talk them into more. Birdie wondered if he had the grace to spare the sisters his obscene jokes about Boston scrod, which were all based on "scrod" being the past tense of a certain verb. "Wanna get scrod? Ha! Ha! Ha!" he'd yell to girls passing by and hold up a filet of the fish.

After Orleans, the streets climbed more steeply. The houses began to get closer together. At this stretch they were mostly wooden triple-deckers with fifteen feet at the most separating them. Then toward the top of the hill was a row of connected brick houses four or five stories tall. On the top two floors of the last house in the row was where the Flynns lived.

An iron fence in bad repair enclosed a small yard in which, years before, somebody in a fit of landscaping zeal had crammed a rhododendron bush, two flowering crab-apple trees and some other unidentifiable bushy thing. It never looked pretty. It only looked cluttered, and Birdie's mother, Marge Flynn, had added to the clutter by sticking in a statue of the Virgin Mary, slightly chipped in the face, that she had bought at some sale. Worst of all, Birdie had been begged, bugged and cajoled by her mother into writing the letter to Mr. Bretz, their landlord, asking permission to do this. Birdie remembered the letter well: "On behalf of my mother, a devout Catholic . . . would like to request . . . in these times of rowdyism [a phrase insisted upon by Marge Flynn and loathed by Birdie] and blasphemy . . . the presence of the figure of our Blessed Mother . . . as a symbol and inspiration . . . ."

Between the blessed weeds of late spring and the tangle of bushes and trees, nobody could really see the statue, anyway. Birdie now went down the cracked walkway that bordered the yard and pulled at the iron bolt that stuck out of the hole in the front door where a doorknob had once been. In the outer hall she checked the row of mailboxes. Theirs was empty. Fowles, Klempster and Wedge still had mail. Then she started up the narrow, winding stairway, passing four different kinds of peeling and stained wallpaper and carpeting that went from burlap to indoor/outdoor to plaid and finally to linoleum—linoleum at the Flynns' entryway.

Birdie got out her key to unlock the door but it opened by itself. She never remembered their faces, just the dark blue serge of their uniforms and the polished metal badges that loomed almost as big as shields in the tight, narrow space of the Flynns' front hall. They could have been the entire police department for all Birdie knew or could feel at that moment when she crossed the threshold. But there were only two officers. She should have had questions but she was too stunned. So she took things in bit by bit—the glaring metal badges, the dark guns embraced by the shiny leather holsters that seemed to ride on their hips at once casually and with a careful show of authority. They must put these on every morning just like I put on underwear, Birdie thought. They brush their teeth, pull on their pants and put on their guns. How weird, she thought, and wondered if their kids watched them while they did it.

"Birdie, you're home. Thank God." Her mother stood there, shapeless and pale in a rose-covered dress and fuzzy white slippers that looked like dead rabbits on her feet. She started to speak again and opened her mouth, but no words came out. Her jaw and chin moved in some spastic motion that could not be coordinated with words. She tried to mouth words but only strangled little sounds came out.

"What is it? What is it, Ma? Is somebody dead?"

"No! No!" her mother almost yelped, and crossed herself, muttering some half-audible prayer.

"Nobody dead, miss," one of the uniforms began. His name tag said SERGEANT COSTELLO. "Your brother Timothy here—" All of a sudden Birdie noticed Timmy. He was standing to one side, handcuffed. "We're arresting him in connection with the vandalism of the Chelsea Street synagogue."

"Timmy, you didn't!"

"Miss, you really shouldn't question your brother here. He is entitled to representation."

To Birdie, Timmy didn't look as if he were entitled to anything. He stood awkwardly, his hands cuffed and his head hung low between his shoulders. He looked absolutely de-titled, if there were such a word.

"We're going down to headquarters," Marge Flynn said.

9

She seemed somewhat more collected. "Your father has been notified." Her voice still trembled but she said "headquarters" and "notified" with that odd inflection she often gave to words that she felt deserved a special respect, words that one usually associated with authority. "We're meeting him there. He's taking off from work."

To all of this, Birdie only had one comment, which she muttered under her breath. She heard her mother say to Sergeant Costello, "I should wash her mouth out with soap." Then Marge Flynn took the dead rabbits off her feet, put on shoes and they all started downstairs. There was an awkward little dance in the narrow hallway as they moved around each other, trying to be very polite while also trying to get out in a reasonably orderly fashion. Then the other sergeant, Sergeant Kempner, started out the door, followed by the handcuffed Timmy, followed by Sergeant Costello, followed by Birdie (wondering if it was hard to walk with handcuffs on), followed by Marge Flynn, who kept rasping at Birdie the whole way down the stairs about her "unladylike" talk and "no respect" and a litany of things that mostly had to do with Birdie's language. Birdie found it only slightly unbelievable that her mother could be going on like this about her swearing when her son was being led away in handcuffs for vandalizing a synagogue.

CHAPTER 2

After they took the handcuffs off, the first thing they did was fingerprint him. Timmy was on the short side, but even a tall person would have had to reach up to be fingerprinted. Everything in the police station seemed designed to make people feel smaller. The ceilings were high, the spaces large and uncluttered. All of the desks were raised so that the officers looked down at whomever approached. In fact, Birdie noticed that the top of the desk where Timmy was being booked reached almost to the officer's shoulders. His head bobbed up and down in a halting rhythm as his arm slowly and laboriously pushed the pen across the paper.

"Name?" he asked flatly.

11

"Timothy Flynn." Birdie noticed that he left out his middle name.

"Current address?"

"Eighty-three Webster Street."

"Age?"

"Seventeen."

The questions went on for another minute or so, and Birdie suddenly realized that Mooch and Skeeter had been brought into the room, with their parents, and that her father had arrived. And then the charge officer read a short statement informing Timmy of his rights and entitlements, but Birdie saw that to the officer Timmy appeared titleless, and that he said the words strictly as a matter of form without any thought or feeling as to meaning. For that single moment they all seemed titleless to Birdie—Timmy in his cowering posture; her mother vague and distracted, moving her lips in a silent echo of the officer's words as if trying to grasp the meaning of what was happening; her father, twitching with rage; and lastly, herself.

The charges were read to all of them: "On the night of June first at eight-thirty, three white males were seen at the front entrance of the Beth Sharon synagogue, 17 Chelsea Street, with cans of spray paint in the act of defacing the doors. . . ."

Here people were distinguished by their crimes, or alleged crimes, Birdie thought, watching the three boys clustered before the desk—Timmy with his sharp features, limp dark hair and thin body; Mooch, slightly taller, with a face that looked as though it had been shoved up from the chin so that his eyes and nose and mouth seemed slammed together into the same plane; and then Skeeter. Skeeter, Birdie thought, her grade-school crush. Red hair, freckles, turned-up nose and blue eyes. He looked like a Kellogg's cereal box kid except for the fact that he was standing in a police station and being charged with vandalizing a synagogue. That their names had been spoken and duly recorded seemed meaningless. How many thousands of names had the sergeant read before in the same colorless voice?

Even their parents looked identical to Birdie, in their slumped postures. Their faces sagged not so much with grimness or sadness but with defeat. Birdie knew that this posture of resignation was nothing new for them. Skeeter's and Mooch's parents, like the Flynns, had stood countless times in the offices of principals and guidance counselors in rituals that informed them of their sons' "inappropriate behavior" or "antisocial behavior." The parents had heard all the special words a hundred times.

A man stepped forward into the harsh light surrounding the charge officer's desk. His mouth was grimly set and he was trembling as he faced the three boys.

"Who are you?" the officer asked, caught off guard.

"Cohen—Stanley Cohen." He tossed the name over his shoulder as if totally uninterested in this charade of formalities being carried out. But suddenly Birdie felt that people were not interchangeable or nameless—here was someone who had a name. The tension in the room was growing.

"I have one question for the boys, officer."

"This is not a formal hearing, sir."

Mr. Cohen ignored him and went on. "I only want to ask them a simple question—"

13

"Sir, I'm going to have to insist—"

"Then I address a question to their parents—the boys can still hear me. Are you familiar with the names Buchenwald? Auschwitz? Bergen-Belsen? Dachau?"

Some of those words Birdie thought she knew, but there was such a deathly sound to Mr. Cohen's voice that whether the names were known or not, a stillness invaded the room. The fingerprint clerk looked up from her files, police officers stopped shuffling their feet and the desk officer took off his glasses. Timmy, Skeeter and Mooch stole glances up from the dirty wooden floor for the first time.

"I say them again: Buchenwald, Auschwitz, Bergen-Belsen, Dachau." He spoke the names in a throaty whisper. It was even more frightening this time.

" 'The Death Camps'—that is what they called them. Many of our congregation, especially the older ones, were in them. They survived them. We do not say, 'Lucky enough to survive.' We say, 'They survived.' One of those survivors is Mrs. Pearlo—" Birdie could not catch the whole name. It sounded like Pearlolit or -litch.

"That Friday night," he continued, "she had sat near the back of the synagogue, which meant that she was one of the first to go up the stairs to leave. She indeed was the first to see your obscenities scrawled across the door. The first to see the swastika—" He stopped now, his mouth half-open in disbelief, his eyes wide as he seemed to envision the woman's horror. He stammered, "C-c-can you imagine? No! No!" He turned to the boys. "You could never imagine. None of you. This woman—she has the numbers tattooed on her." His voice rose and he stabbed at his own arm. "Numbers tattooed on her arm!"

He turned and left.

As soon as they were out the door of the station, her father had Timmy by the elbow and was yanking him and shouting at him at the top of his lungs. Birdie was still thinking about Mrs. Pearlo-what. She was trying as hard as she had ever tried to imagine this woman's shock when she came up the stairs and saw the glass door. Did she see it all at once as she climbed the stairs, or did small parts of the sprayed writing become visible to her one at a time and then begin to fit together like pieces in some horrible puzzle? Did she scream? Had Mr. Cohen said she screamed? Birdie imagined a scream, or did she just imagine the shape of a scream on the woman's mouth, which seemed scarier than an actual scream? Birdie's thoughts were abruptly interrupted. Marge and Timmy were hurtling down the station steps toward the sidewalk. Joe Flynn had exploded with a swing at Timmy that had caught Marge, too, and they both went flying.

CHAPTER
3

What a tangled-up, messed-up family. That is what Birdie thought each time she pictured the scene at the bottom of the station steps with her mother and Timmy sprawled and dazed, her father still cursing and trying to help his wife up. Somehow, Birdie had wound up standing next to Mr. Cohen, who just looked down at the tangled mess, shaking his head.

It was Saturday morning, two weeks since going to the police station, three days since the hearing, but Birdie kept reliving the scenes. She lay in bed hearing again the eerie cadences of Mr. Cohen's voice as he recited the camp names, which had become like a litany playing in the background of the scenes. She imagined the writing as it appeared to Mrs.

16

Pearlo-what on the glass doors, then her mother tumbling down the stairs, only to rise unsteadily to her feet, protesting the whole time, "I'm fine. I'm fine. I know it was for Timmy, not me. For Timmy."

For Timmy—all of it was for Timmy. But this time it was different. It seemed to be for all of them including Birdie, even though she had nothing to do with what had happened on Chelsea Street on June 1. In some odd way, the whole family seemed caught in it.

Now Birdie could not think of one good reason to get out of bed. By next Saturday she would be working at Filene's basement, the demolition derby of clothing, a bargain hunter's delight, if one had the stamina to fight off the hordes. Once Birdie had seen a Jacques Cousteau movie about the feeding frenzy of sharks, and it reminded her exactly of Filene's basement, especially when the designer jeans went on sale. All the best names went for almost nothing: Calvin Klein, Gloria Vanderbilt, Sasson, Jordache. A week ago she would have been thrilled with her store discount and the prospect of loading up on jeans with Gloria Saccharelli, who would also be working in the basement. True, she would not be selling jeans but working at the separates counter, which meant the double-knit crowd, which was, she supposed, the same as the double-chin crowd. They wouldn't be in the basement forever. She and Gloria had plans for advancement straight up to designer sportswear on the fourth floor. But none of it excited her anymore. It wasn't as if everything had changed since Timmy's arrest. Very little had changed and maybe that was the problem, not just with her but with the whole family.

Maybe the Flynns weren't smart enough to change. Maybe they would go on like this forever. Birdie groaned and buried her head in her pillow—that was the worst.

"Are you going to eat anything this morning?" Marge Flynn yelled through Birdie's closed door.

Birdie rolled over and stretched. "All right! All right! Coming."

The bedroom door opened a little. A young woman's face peeked around.

"When you start work, Birdie?" The face was a perfect heart shape, very pale, the color of raw dough, and one eye was black and blue and sealed shut to a slit. The pale blond hair was in rollers.

"Lainie!" Birdie squinted at her elder sister. "What happened to you?"

"Richie."

"You here with Rhonda?" What she really wanted to ask was why anybody would go to the trouble of putting her hair in rollers when she had a black eye from her husband.

"Yeah. Any objection?"

"Why would I object? Don't get touchy."

"Ma wants to know what you want for breakfast."

"Just coffee."

Marge Flynn always kept the shades drawn in the kitchen, which faced the harbor and the morning sun. The only light this morning, aside from the fixture above the table, was blue gray that poured from the black-and-white portable television. Rhonda, Lainie's four-year-old, was watching the

Flintstones. Not quite awake yet, Birdie stopped to watch Rhonda watch the Flintstones, who were watching television on their cave TV set. It suddenly struck her as rather odd, like the picture on the salt box of the girl with the umbrella in the rain holding a box with the same picture of a girl with an umbrella holding a box and on to infinity. Here she was in a box watching someone watch another box watching another family watching another box. What were the Flintstones watching, she wondered?

"Cute, isn't it?" Marge said as she slid a mug of coffee into Birdie's hand and stood next to her to watch.

"Not particularly."

"Well, personally I like the Flintstones. I think it's very educational—all about cave men."

"Mother, it's not. It gives all the wrong information. Cave people didn't have television and go bowling."

"You're so snobby, Birdie," Lainie muttered.

"Well, they're a lovely family," Marge said. As opposed to us, thought Birdie.

> *A is for apple,*
> *J is for jacks.*
> *Cinnamon toasty Applejacks.*

A commercial. Rhonda kept watching. Birdie went and sat down at the kitchen table. "Can't she watch on the set in the living room?"

"I can't." The spell was broken. "Grandpa's still asleep in the bedroom and it will wake him up," Rhonda whined. "What did Aunt Birdie do to her eyebrows?"

"Never mind," Birdie said.

"She tried to pluck them like that sexpot Paris Wells."

"Mother, she's not a sexpot. She's a model and an actress."

"She's a *w-h-o-r-e*," spelled Marge, but Rhonda was already back with the Flintstones, watching them watch the mastodon Derby at the rock track. Marge was watching, too, now. "What's a mastodon?" she said to no one in particular.

Lainie snorted. "A whore—that's what she says about everyone who's not a nun." This brought Marge back quickly from the rock track and the mastodons.

"Watch your tongue, Lainie!"

This was a touchy subject between mother and daughter. It had been Marge Flynn's hope that Lainie would become a nun, until she got pregnant in her junior year of high school and had to marry Richie.

"Well, it's going to take more than eyebrows to make Birdie look like Paris Wells. You look ridiculous with those bushy slants over your eyes."

"It's better than what Richie did to yours."

"Shut up!" spat Lainie.

"Both of you shut up!" screamed Marge.

"You know what I really and truly want?" A little voice came out of the wash of light. "I really want the Walk-Around Farm from Hasbro's Romper Room, each part sold separately, no assembly required." Rhonda's tiny voice was a calm and distinct echo of the TV toy commercial.

"Oh, lovey." Marge hugged her granddaughter. "I'll get it for you for your birthday."

Joe Flynn walked into the kitchen and sat down in a chair

by the window. He moved the shade slightly and looked out. "Where's Timmy? Down at the piers?"

"No, in his room," Marge said.

"Oh, Jeez!" Lainie sighed. "This again!"

"What do you mean, 'this again,' Lainie?" Joe shouted at his daughter. "This is with us for a while."

Birdie looked up from her coffee cup. Dr. Doom was blasting Spiderman with twin lasers beaming from his eyes. Would Spiderman's net hold up?

"You think it will just go away, don't you, Lainie?"

"No, I don't. But I think that you're all making an awfully big deal over it. I mean, it's not like he killed somebody or raped some kid."

"Lainie!" screeched Marge. "Not in front of Rhonda!" Rhonda could have cared less. Dr. Doom's laser eyes were splintering a skyscraper.

"Well," Lainie continued, "you've got to get on with your life, you know."

What life? Birdie thought, and felt a thick depression settle over her. Timmy walked into the room. He had heard Lainie's remark, and Birdie knew that he was probably thinking the same thing she was.

"Timmy," Joe said, looking scornfully at his son. "I went to my boss last night—Mr. Goldman. He'd been out of town so he hadn't seen the *Globe*. I say to him, 'Mr. Goldman,' I say . . . ." A sickening feeling washed over Birdie. If her father had been fired, that was the end. Marge must have been thinking the same thing. She plunged her hand into the pocket of her housecoat and pulled out a pack of cigarettes. It was empty. Marge crunched it up and got a new pack from her purse. The rasp of cellophane and small noises of cigarettes being opened were familiar sounds against the screams and clashes coming from the television. " 'I don't want you to hear about this from anyone else,' " Joe continued, "and then I tell him what happened. And when I tell him, you know what he says to me?"

Timmy looked down and shook his head. The rustle of the cigarette pack in Marge's hands seemed to chip away at the noises coming from the television. "He says, 'Joe,' he says, 'What is your son? Is he mental?' "

"What did you say, Joe?" Marge whispered.

"I say, 'No, he ain't mental. As far as I know it was just a prank.' "

Prank. Birdie and Timmy both looked at each other when Joe said the word. To Birdie it seemed an odd word to use. She wondered if Timmy didn't think so, too.

"You're not fired, are you, Joe?"

"For Crissakes, no, Marge! Where else are they going to find some jerk to wrestle furniture fourteen hours a day to support a wife, kids and grandchild?" He turned to Lainie. "Richie rough you up again?"

"Yeah."

The phone rang. "Don't you get it, Birdie," Marge yelled. "I'll get it." There had been a series of phone calls since the write-up in the paper, mostly from right-wing groups anxious to attach themselves to a good cause.

"Yes. Yes." Marge nodded as she spoke into the receiver. "Just a minute." She covered the mouthpiece with her hand.

"It's for Timmy. It's a young man. He sounds very nice. Very polite."

"They all sound nice at first, Marge."

"I'll take it." Timmy reached for the phone.

Everybody was watching Timmy, who listened intently until his mouth hardened and his eyes looked defiant again, losing the glazed look they had had for days. "No. I told you before. I wouldn't be interested. No. Not at all." He hung up the phone.

"Who was it?" they all asked at once.

"Nobody."

"Goddammit! It was somebody," Joe yelled. "Now who the hell was it?"

"Don't talk to me like that!" Timmy shot back.

Joe started for Timmy. He got him around the chest with one arm. Joe Flynn's arms were huge from moving furniture all day. He crushed Timmy tighter. Birdie hated it when he did this to Timmy. She always waited to hear his ribs crack, just crunch up like chicken bones in the disposal. "Who was it?" Joe yelled.

Tell him, Birdie prayed. Tell him before I hear the awful cracks.

> *A is for apple,*
> *J is for jacks.*
> *Cinnamon toasty....*

"The American Nazi Party!" Timmy blurted out. "They still want me to come to a recruitment meeting."

He broke loose and faced his parents, his eyes dancing with

rage. "They say I can enter their junior officer training program. Isn't that great? I could carry a card. You know, like Birdie has an ID for Filene's. And maybe I'd get a diploma, too. Especially since I won't be getting one from school, Ma. You're always talking about how the Hallorans have all their kids' diplomas up in the kitchen and you don't have any from your kids."

His raw voice cut the air. They all stared at him. Joe turned with an oath and abruptly left the room. Lainie looked as if she had just eaten something vaguely distasteful. Rhonda drifted back to the TV and yawned as some creature on "Road Runner" was flayed out of his skin and then miraculously zipped into it again. But Marge's eyes were filled with tears. She seemed hypnotized by the hoarse, trembling boy in front of her.

"Is that what you want from me, Ma? Is that what you want?" He yelled again and again at her, as if the only energy he had left was for rage and destruction.

"Stop it! Stop it!" Birdie screamed.

Timmy tore out of the apartment. She knew where he was going—to the piers. It was the one place a person could think calmly if they lived in the Flynn household.

CHAPTER
4

She saw him at the end of the pier. His legs were hanging over the edge and his head was up, looking straight ahead, looking at nothing. That was the difference between her and Timmy. He looked across the harbor and saw nothing. She looked across and saw lights. It had always been this way when they came to the piers to talk and be silent and just be together, away from their crazy family and the television. It was the quiet that they both liked. But for Birdie the piers were a beginning and for Timmy they were an end.

She hadn't told him half of what she thought about the other side, about her plans with Gloria. He'd listen to some of it and sometimes smile quietly. He never said much about her dreams. He was no dreamer. No dreamer, she thought, as she looked at him now. He had an oddly inanimate face that had, Birdie felt, a rather interesting structure. His high cheekbones made his eyes appear more deeply set than they actually were. His face was thin, but big boned, with a sharply angled jaw and the cheekbones flattened into interesting planes around his eyes and temples. But it was an oddly inexpressive face that seemed almost carved. Shadows and light were caught by the sharp planes, but no light radiated from the eyes.

They did not speak for a long time, but sat quietly, Timmy looking straight down at the black water filmed with patches of oil. The gaudy swirls of color were strangely hypnotic. Birdie looked east toward the mouth of the harbor and Castle Island to the south. Slowly, her eyes swept west toward the waterfront renovation—the jutting piers of India Wharf with its splendid new aquarium; Long Wharf with its old coffee and chocolate warehouses, now renovated into elegant condominiums; then Commercial, Lewis, Sargent's and Union wharfs, which had been stripped of the old smells of sea trade and bait and now housed people, boutiques, offices and restaurants.

That's where the jeans were, Birdie thought, and the designer shoes and bags and all the stuff that had signatures and initials, those stamps of style and taste and belonging. She was determined not to spend all of her salary on clothes, just some, enough to spruce up her image for promotional purposes. She might start in the basement, but by the time she reached designer sportswear she hoped to have enough money saved and a good enough salary to share an apartment with Gloria on the other side. That was the real goal: to get out of that crazy household, to really get out and not just always be

26

sitting on the pier staring across at what she wanted. It wouldn't be a wharf condo—she and Gloria could never afford that—but it would be over there—something small and stylish.

Birdie's thoughts rushed ahead to wicker and hanging plants. But something had begun to happen to the vivid images of life across the harbor. The harder she thought about them, the more elusive they seemed. She looked again at Timmy, the carved face with eyes that seemed not to see, seemed never to dream. As always, those eyes were looking straight ahead. As always, she was sitting next to him, but the images were growing dimmer and dimmer. She was afraid now. She began to talk rapidly as if to resuscitate whatever it was that was dying.

"I'm not going to blow my whole salary on designer jeans," she said.

"Oh, really?" Timmy looked at her for the first time. "What are you going to blow it on? An encyclopedia set?"

"Don't make fun of me," she snapped. "No. I'm going to get one of those linen blazers, slightly flared." Birdie didn't know why she was going into such fashion detail with Timmy. "It'll go with everything, and I'll look more like a department buyer than a clerk. A blazer will take me a lot further than a pair of designer jeans." She said this almost fiercely.

"Franchise dreams," Timmy muttered.

"What? What are you talking about?"

"I mean that if McDonald's sold dreams you'd buy one. That's what those dreams and the rest of it are—franchise dreams."

"It's better than no dreams," Birdie replied grimly, thinking that Timmy could speak quite well when he felt like it. Timmy went back to staring at the iridescent swirls of color filming the water.

"What's going to happen about you and school, Timmy?"

"Nothing. I'm out. The last straw, the last chance."

"You sound relieved."

"No. I'm just out. It's a simple fact."

"There're other ways. Freddie Ferraro got back in last year."

"His old man put on the pressure." Somehow, Birdie could not imagine their father pressuring the authorities.

"Well, there's that high school equivalency stuff."

"I'm not equivalent," Timmy half laughed.

"Timmy!" She was used to him talking this way, but it seemed intolerable now.

"Forget it, Birdie. Besides, I've got to work to pay off the fine. They made that all clear in the hearing. Court costs, damages, fine paid within the year. No messing around."

He was quiet again. It might have been a minute, no more, but within that minute she had sensed it coming, something they had been talking around up to now. Except at the hearings, Timmy had not said a word about the incident since that day in the station. Then again, their father and mother had never asked him any questions. There had been the usual rhetorical *Why?* questions, but before he could answer, which Birdie doubted he would anyway, their father would start yelling at him, their mother crying and praying, and Timmy would not have to speak, could not speak even if he wanted to. They all had their roles to play, which had little to do with what was actually going on. Timmy had given the expected response, the only response possible amid the noise and abuses, the prayers and the television, which was "I don't know." He then withdrew into a sullen silence that was not so much a defense but a submission.

Conversation did not come easy in the Flynn household. Attempting to talk with another person was like running an obstacle course, and it was easier to give up than go the distance. So Birdie had not expected any words from Timmy in the apartment about that night on Chelsea Street. She knew that if she were going to hear anything about it, it would be most likely at the piers.

"It wasn't me. Skeeter and Mooch did the really bad stuff."

So he didn't write anything on the doors. So what? thought Birdie—was he really going to blame it all on Skeeter and Mooch? There was much more to it and even if her family hadn't asked the details and even if Lainie thought it was all going to go away, Birdie wanted to know. She wanted to know every little thing about that night.

"So you didn't write anything with the spray cans?"

"Well, yeah, but no words," Timmy said uncertainly. "Look, Birdie. I mean, it's not like I'm the first person to ever do anything like this. For years Ma and Dad have sat around taking pot shots at Mr. Goldman."

"I know, but it's not the same thing."

"It is, too, the same thing. What about you? You laughed when Dad would do his imitations. You joked about it and you never said nothing when Dad talked about the Jews taking over. . . ."

Birdie moved uncomfortably. "Well, that was wrong—"

there ever was a jerk, it's Goldman.''

s a jerk, I know, but there are other jerks around.
k at Joe T.''

"What are we talking about him for?''

"You can be a jerk without being Jewish, Timmy. Look at us, for instance.'' She was startled by the bitterness in her own voice.

"Man, I don't know what you're talking about.''

Birdie wasn't sure herself. Timmy had begun speaking quickly. He was saying something about how he had just made marks with the spray. "Just some marks,'' he kept saying. "Just some stupid little marks.''

"There was a swastika up there,'' Birdie said, watching the harbor.

"I didn't do that. I swear. Mooch did that one. Mine were just squiggles and slashes—you know, marks. All this hassle over some meaningless marks, for God's sake. We didn't hurt nobody.''

"Meaningless,'' Birdie said, and began to wonder again about Mrs. Pearlo-what. When did the marks become meaningful to her as she came up the stairs and saw the glass door? Where did the meaning begin for the old lady with the numbers on her arm?

"Yeah,'' Timmy was saying. "You know, not any bad names. You know what I mean.''

"Yeah,'' Birdie said tiredly. "I know what you mean.'' But she wasn't sure that she did.

They sat quietly for a little longer. A tugboat a hundred yards or so offshore began to swing sharply toward the pier where Birdie and Timmy were sitting. They both were startled, as boats seldom pulled up to this particular pier. It was soon apparent by the uneven sound of the engine that there was a problem.

"It's not a Boston Company boat," Timmy said, noticing the green and white colors of the stack. "It must be an independent."

"They're coming right toward us." Birdie started to get up.

"I know. What are we supposed to do?"

"How should I know?"

The engine cut off suddenly, and there was only the sound of the boat's first bow waves slapping the pilings of the pier.

"Hey, you kids!" A man leaned out of a porthole of the wheelhouse. "We got trouble here. Lost our engine. The tide will take us if we don't get tied up."

Both Birdie and Timmy stood stock still. It flashed into Birdie's mind that in all the years of going to the piers they had never spoken to any of the harbor people.

"You kids!" His voice was more urgent now. "One of you get forward and one aft on the pier."

The captain was shooting rapid-fire instructions. A small, wiry woman dashed back and forth between bow and stern, readying the dock lines. She mounted a forward bollard post and stood poised with a length of rope in her hands. She was set to cast the bow line. Birdie looked at Timmy. He appeared paralyzed.

"I'll catch this one, Timmy, but you get ready for the other one. Okay, Timmy?" Heart pounding, Birdie gave him a shove down the pier and turned back toward the tug.

Like a discus thrower, the woman rotated her small body

on top of the bollard and heaved. A serpentine of rope came sailing out of the blue sky. The knot at the end began a smooth, graceful plummet toward Birdie. She looked up and raised her arms. She felt her heart beat even faster, and then there was the solid thunk of the rope at her feet. She grabbed it quickly. "Take a turn on the piling," the woman shouted, and raced toward the stern. The language was unfamiliar. For a fleeting moment, Birdie thought the woman wanted her to get on top of the piling and do a slow twirl as she herself had done when throwing the rope. Then Birdie realized that she was suppose to make the rope fast, and she scrambled to cast a loop over the head of the post. She tried once, missed, and tried again and made it. She pulled hard on the rope. It seemed to hold. Excitedly, she looked down the pier for Timmy.

The stern swung out dangerously as the ebb caught it. The woman shouted instructions to Timmy but he appeared not to hear. Birdie saw the woman twist her body once more atop the bollard. The rotation was tighter. The heaving had to be more powerful if the rope was to reach, but Timmy had not even raised his arms. Time seemed nearly to stop. The people, the boat, even the water became like a film in slow motion. Within the slow, viscous movement of the scene, Birdie tried to will her brother to raise his arms, to move, to act. All meaning seemed to be condensed into this single moment, all chances to be taken now. For Birdie it seemed that within this moment life, chance, risk and meaning telescoped suddenly and Timmy stood frozen in the crosshairs of his fate.

"For once in your life, Timmy," Birdie muttered desperately, caught somewhere between prayer and a command. "For once in your life . . . ."

32

CHAPTER 5

"And tomorrow you can mop out those restrooms in the parish house, and we'll see about vacuuming the pews. Although, personally, I'm against it. And remember, you don't go near the altar. Father Leo says no way you go near that altar, kid. And I report directly to him and I'll knock the . . . ."

The stale air of the church basement was laced with the abusive voice. At first, its high, squeaky tone seemed so peculiar to Birdie that she thought it might be that of a child having a tantrum. She walked down the hall and stood quietly outside the janitor's room of Our Lady of Victory. No victories to be racked up here, she nearly said aloud. But it was a job. The money was decent, and Timmy would be able to pay back their father for the lawyer's fees. No use being polite about interrupting this, Birdie thought. She took a deep breath and strode into the middle of the high-pitched tirade.

A wave of nausea swept over Birdie as she stepped into the room. Directly before her was Timmy, his head bowed in front of a squealing man-baby. Scarlet from his ranting, the pudgy man swallowed hard and wet his lips as if to regain a more fitting composure. The voice was still high, but decorous, his color less florid.

"Good afternoon, miss. What may I do for you? I'm Benny Arlette, sacristan of Our Lady of Victory."

Birdie's first instinct was to squeeze his fat, little neck until he turned purple. A thin line of spittle ran from the corner of his baby-doll mouth. Birdie focused hard on it. So this is Timmy's boss, she thought. And this was his work—mopping toilets and taking crap from Benny Arlette. Her throat constricted as she remembered the scene on the pier just two days ago when Timmy, as if an electric current had suddenly coursed through his body, leaped high into the air and met the rope against the clear blueness of the sky—catching the serpent by the throat with a move stunning both in its power and grace.

"I'm Bridget Flynn."

Benny's small eyes stretched open wider. "Oh, this one's sister?"

Birdie did not answer. She turned her back on him.

"Come on, Timmy. You'll be late for your interview with Captain Petersen. He really wants you to come down to the pier right away." It was, of course, a lie, a complete and total fabrication, but Birdie's words came like that rope sailing out of the blue for Timmy. Raising his head and lively with a new energy, he quickly said, "Oh! I nearly forgot, Benny. I've got an appointment."

The fat face dissolved into puddles of confusion. The eyes flinched with a dull light. Pig winks, Birdie thought, and the little mouth twisted and curled, trying to form words. "I . . . I . . . I told you to call me Mr. Arlette. Only Father Leo calls me . . . ."

"Oh, sorry," Timmy said casually as he swung out the door. "Mr. Arlette it is, if that's what pleases."

And together Birdie and Timmy ran down the basement corridor and out the alley exit of Our Lady of Victory.

> *Strawberry shortcake,*
> *Huckleberry pie,*
> *V-I-C-T-O-R-Y.*

It was an old grade-school cheer that rang in her brain and set a rhythm for Birdie's feet on the pavement. But the cheer stopped. The rhythm ceased. They had squelched Benny, that was true, and that was all. Poking holes, however, in miserable excuses for human beings was not a victory, at least not the kind Birdie imagined. They slowed now to a walk. She felt embarrassed about her inclination to inflate a put-down into a victory. She knew that Timmy would never think of it in those terms. She wondered, however, what he did think of her lie to Benny. He certainly had picked up the cue quickly enough.

"Maybe it is worth a try," Birdie thought aloud.

"What's worth a try?" Timmy asked.

"The Petersens. Maybe you should go over there and see if they need somebody like you. They did say their deckhand just quit."

"Like me?" Timmy laughed. "I doubt it."

She hated it when he spoke this way.

"Look, Timmy, when the crunch came you caught the rope, made it fast better than I did and threw the tail back to Mrs. Petersen—something I never thought of doing. You did it perfectly. They said so. They were clearly more impressed with you than with me. They're neat people, good people. They're not going to get their kicks like Benny Fat-Face over there, grinding you down."

"Yeah, but that was a lucky catch. I might botch it, and I'd rather botch it for Benny Arlette than for the Petersens."

"Oh," said Birdie flatly, as if this were supposed to make some sort of sense, which it didn't. Sometimes she just did not know how to reach Timmy, how to talk to him. It was as if she were continually trying to follow him down streets that wound up being dead ends. They walked on for a while in silence.

"Timmy!" Birdie scuffed her shoes along the sidewalk. "You're doing it again."

"What?" Timmy moved slightly ahead of her, jamming his fists into the pockets of his jacket.

They walked in more silence. Birdie took a breath and moved faster to catch up.

"I just don't understand why you can't take a chance once in a while." She was horrified to hear her voice waver, and she angrily cleared her throat. Timmy laughed uneasily.

"Why pass up a sure bet?" he said.

"Don't laugh, Timmy." Birdie was almost shouting. "Sureness isn't such a great thing. Sureness is for old people who live in those retirement places in Arizona who want to make sure every day is sunny with no chance of rain." Birdie felt the tears coming and relentlessly forced them away. "Timmy, all your life you've been watching those boats, loving those boats."

"I don't know anything about boats, though."

"You don't know anything about Benny Arlette either, except that he's a jerk, and you sure don't want to know anything about cleaning out the church. Timmy, take a risk on something you at least like."

Timmy looked out across the water, then down at the ground. He kicked a soda can with his foot.

"I'll think about it, okay?"

She knew he said it more to stop the conversation than anything else. They walked on silently for another half block.

"So how was Filene's?"

"Okay for a first day, I guess."

"You and Gloria in the same place?"

"No, I'm in separates and she's in Big Lady lingerie."

"Big Lady?"

"Yeah. For sizes twenty and up—bras, girdles. It's more like steel-beam construction."

"Huh, and skinny Gloria's selling to these heavy weights."

"Yep. You can't say that Filene's is into psychology."

"Guess not."

They turned into their walkway. The chipped madonna

peered out from behind an old rhododendron blossom. It was nearly six o'clock and everybody would be home, including Rhonda.

Here he comes to save the day.
Mighty Mouse is on the way!

The Mighty Mouse theme song swirled down the stairs to greet them as they reached the landing and headed up the last flight. They both took a deep breath before they walked through the apartment door.

"Ha!" Joe set down his beer. "Did you go to your job?"

"Where'd you think I've been?" Timmy replied.

"Don't give me any lip."

Birdie walked by them and plopped on the couch next to Rhonda, who, despite her glazed appearance, acknowledged Birdie's arrival. "Watch this, Aunt Birdie. Mighty Mouse is going to smash through that thing and pick up that television tower and fly off with it."

Why couldn't their father have just said to Timmy, "How was your job?" instead of, "Did you go to your job?" Why even wonder? she thought. She stared ahead at the TV. Sure enough, Mighty Mouse was flying through the air holding an entire television tower in front of him like a lance. "How did you know that he was going to get that tower, Rhonda?"

"Me and Michelle seen this one before. He's so cute, that Mighty Mouse," she cooed.

"Oh, God," muttered Birdie, thinking that Mighty Mouse must be the Burt Reynolds of the under-six set.

"How was work, Timmy? Did you see Father Leo?" Marge

walked in from the kitchen with a bowl in the crook of her arm. She was stirring something thick. "Did you tell him you're the son of Marge Enright Flynn and . . . ."

"I haven't seen him yet." Timmy cut her off abruptly.

"Haven't seen him yet? Well, why not?"

"Look, Ma, I mop out the restrooms, clean the toilets, take out the trash, wash the basement windows—not the stained glass. Besides, he'd hardly remember me. It's been almost ten years since my first communion." A bitter edge had crept into Timmy's voice. Birdie's hand reached for Rhonda's. They both stared ahead into the TV and watched Mighty Mouse's closing battle. "You ain't going to find Father Leo swabbing cans."

"Watch your language, Timmy!" Joe spoke sharply from behind his paper.

"Pardon me—toilets."

Joe lowered the paper and glared at Timmy.

"Well, who tells you what to do?" Marge asked. "Who do you work for?"

"Benny Arlette."

"That half-wit?" Marge said weakly.

"A half-wit for a quarter-wit," Joe chuckled from behind his paper. "What's for dinner, Marge?"

"Bluefish."

"You buy it from that creep Joe T.?"

"No, I got it at the Stop & Shop."

"Good. I don't want to catch you near that creep." He got up to get another beer from the kitchen.

"What? You don't trust me?" she yelled after him.

"I trust you," he shouted over his shoulder. "It's the creep I don't trust." Marge looked as if she did not know whether to feel pleased or exasperated by his concern.

"Cripes, Dad." Birdie turned on the couch. "What do you think he's going to do? Attack Ma right there in Maverick Square, on the ice bed in the back of the truck with the little neck clams and the flounder?"

"You shut your mouth, missy, before you get a slap." Joe was pointing at her menacingly with his hand that held the beer. A little slopped over the edge. "You don't go interfering into marital relations—understand?"

"Come on, Aunt Birdie. It's time for 'The Brady Bunch.' They're going on their vacation to the Grand Canyon."

"I might puke," Birdie said, and got up and stomped into her room. She burrowed deep into her sweater drawer and pulled out a notebook. She sat down on her bed, took out the ballpoint pen she kept stuck in the spiral binding and began to write.

Why do they call me "missy"? It only happens once in a while, but it really bugs me when it does. I'd rather have them call me "jerk" or "stupid" or anything else almost. Come to think of it, they call me missy at very special times—like when I look smarter than them, or try to challenge them on their own ground. They don't call me missy when I complain about going to the laundromat or even the time I cut school with Gloria. No, they call me missy when they think I know something that I shouldn't know—like about marital relations or sex. They call me missy to make me feel like a little girl—a powerless little girl. They call Rhonda missy, too. All the time, whether they're mad at her or not. And Ma, she's a missy sometimes to Dad, even though he might not call her that. Like tonight when he went on with all that stuff about Joe T. Ma, she didn't know whether to be glad to be a missy or angry to be a woman. That came out funny, the way I put it. I'm not sure if you have to be angry to be a woman, but, my God, she's forty-four years old and she's still letting him tell her where to buy fish! My father is truly a slob. [She stopped here and chewed on her pen a moment, then decided to cross it out.]

I hate the Brady Bunch. I shouldn't but I do. I know they aren't real, but are we real? I mean, like what is a family? Is it all this sweetness-and-light crap with cheery moms and patient and wise dads and cute kids and a stream of jokes? I mean, that can't be real. But how real can we be?

That was all she could think to write at the moment. She closed the notebook. There was a soft knock at the door.

"Who is it?"

"Lainie."

"Come in."

Lainie was carrying a small, pink vinyl case.

"What's that?" Birdie asked.

"My Carol Beth sample kit." Her face was unusually animated. "I'm in the cosmetics business."

"You're what?"

"In the cosmetics business."

41

"What do you do?"

"Sell cosmetics—the Carol Beth line of superior beauty and skin-care products."

"Door to door?"

"And over the phone and at Carol Beth beauty parties when I get to be a district manager."

"Oh, let me see the kit," Birdie asked excitedly.

"I want to see, too." Marge came into Birdie's room.

Lainie carefully opened the kit's top.

"Oooh!" Birdie and her mother both exclaimed. There were myriads of little pots, tubes, vials and bottles. There were fifteen different lipsticks arranged in three different ranks, five to a row, ranging from soft pinks to violent reds. There were round cakes of blushers with names like Tawny Sunset or Desert Light. There was even one called Wine Dark, which made Birdie wonder if Carol Beth was not secretly a Greek scholar underneath her Exuberanza moisturizer and Red-As-All-Get-Out lipstick. There were also bright rectangles of eyeshadow and skinny gold tubes of eyeliner.

"Better not let Rhonda get hold of this. She'd love messing around with it."

"I sneaked in with it. She's out there with Dad watching the news."

News, cartoons, thought Birdie. It's all the same to Rhonda.

"Oh, Lainie"—Marge was studying a long piece of paper—"is this an order form?"

"Yeah."

"But, Lainie, this looks difficult to do. Look, you have to figure tax and everything."

"She can do it, Ma."

"I don't know, Birdie. She has to figure state tax, and what's this commission column on items over six dollars and mailing charges? I don't think Lainie can do this sort of higher mathematics."

Birdie saw Lainie's face start to change. It didn't exactly droop. It just became less animated and then still. The pallid, doughy skin seemed flaccid once more.

"She can do it. I'll lend her my calculator."

"I don't know," Marge said, getting up from the corner of the bed. "It could be a real disaster."

"Maybe she's right," Lainie said. "And besides, Richie's not going to like this at all. I'll have to hide it from him."

"Then, if you have to hide it," Marge said, walking out the door and waving her hand in a gesture of dismissal, "you shouldn't do it. In marital relations, everything should be up front. Marriage must be based on honesty, not deceit."

"Welcome to the Ann Landers Institute of Marital Relations," said Birdie. "East Boston Branch."

"Don't go getting fresh, missy." There it was again, that word. "I know my children's limitations and I just try to protect them."

"Does the Brady Bunch have limitations?"

"Birdie, what in heaven's name are you talking about?"

"Nothing."

Marge left. As soon as she was gone, Birdie got up and closed the door, motioning for Lainie to stay. "You can keep the kit here so Richie won't see it. Just put it in the second drawer over there and when you need it, come and get it. With the calculator you'll have no problems."

"Thanks, Birdie. I don't know why you're doing this."

"I don't, either," Birdie said honestly. "What are you going to do with all the money you'll make?"

"Gee, I don't know. Maybe save for a divorce." She said this in much the same way as one might say, "Save for a rainy day."

The door opened. "Ma." Rhonda peeked in.

Birdie quickly threw a blouse over the kit. "Ma, can we go to a participating McDonald's for dinner?"

"Sure, honey."

"A participating McDonald's!" Birdie repeated.

"Yeah," said Rhonda.

"You are the complete video child, Rhonda. How would you like to go on an actual real-life experience sometime?"

"What's that?"

"You know, one real-life experience not brought to you by Ideal Toy or Milton Bradley."

"Brought by what?" Rhonda asked.

"By me—your kind, old auntie—me and"—Birdie said with sudden inspiration—"and the Boston parks."

"What do they make?" Rhonda asked. Her pale, heart-shaped face was full of skepticism.

"Swan boats—no assembly required. The last day of school I get out early and we'll go for a swan-boat ride in the public gardens."

"Is it like the Grand Canyon?"

"No. It's nothing like the Grand Canyon, Rhonda, and the Brady Bunch won't be there. It's you and me in the Boston Public Gardens being paddled on a big pond with real live ducks."

"Okay. I'll do it!" Rhonda said with real excitement.

44

Down at the piers after dinner Birdie and Timmy sat quietly. The sky was streaked pink and mauve, almost the same colors as the rectangles of eyeshadow in the Carol Beth sample kit. The air was quite clear, and against the iridescent colors of the sky the buildings appeared even darker and seemed to lose their dimensionality. They looked almost unreal, like paper cutouts. So much seemed unreal to Birdie.

"Do you think it was a 'prank,' like they keep saying?"

Timmy waited several seconds to answer. "Do you mean, do I think it was a joke or real?"

"I guess that's what I mean."

"Well, it wasn't real. I mean, not that we had anything against those people, but it's hard to think of it like a joke now, either."

"Yeah," Birdie said, in her mind seeing Mrs. Pearlo-what coming up the stairs.

"You know," Timmy went on, "it all just sort of happened that night. It's real hard to explain. I don't know whose idea it was. It wasn't even exactly an idea. Maybe more like a feeling or something that came over us all together at once and just grew."

Birdie stared down at the water as Timmy was speaking and watched it wash against the pilings.

"It was just there and we did it, I guess," Timmy said.

"That's what climbers say about mountains, Timmy—because it's there." Birdie got up and started walking home.

That night Birdie sat out on the fire escape on the harbor side of the building, writing in her notebook.

Timmy keeps talking about how the idea just sort of grew as if it had some life and will of its own, and every time he starts doing this I start looking down at the water washing against the pilings. Tonight it was an incoming tide, and there was something about those waves that started me thinking: Does a wave know it's going to crash eventually? What could interrupt its path? Delay it? Make it break away from the tide? Mooch, Skeeter and Timmy— is that what they were that night—waves of a tide? No will? No singleness? It's scary to think about. Maybe we're all like this dirty water sloshing in and out of Boston Harbor, bossed by the moon.

CHAPTER
6

"So you see, Rhonda, there was this family of ducks, and the little ducklings had just hatched and they'd all been living in the Charles River, but they needed to find a permanent home." Rhonda and Birdie had just switched trains at Park Street to catch the Red Line to Charles in an attempt to retrace as much as possible Mr. and Mrs. Mallard's walk from the river to the Public Gardens as it was told in the famous picture book. But Rhonda did not seem all that interested in the literary background of her first real-life experience.

"I thought you said it was real. Did the policeman really stop traffic for the ducks?"

"No, it's a story, silly. They read it to me when I was in nursery school, and we went and took a swan-boat ride where the ducks in the story were supposed to have gone to live.''

"Then it's not real," said Rhonda stubbornly.

"The swan boats are real and the pond is real and there are real mallard ducks on the pond. The guy who wrote the book drew pictures of things that really are here. My teacher told us he made the story up from some newspaper article he read. It's much more real than that Mighty Mouse crap on television.''

"There really are mice, too, you know!''

There was no winning with this kid, Birdie thought. She should just shut up and hope that Rhonda liked the swan-boat ride.

They entered through the gate at the corner of Beacon and Charles streets and headed diagonally across the gardens toward the pond. They had only gone a few yards when Rhonda stopped to watch three children chasing squirrels in and out of the pools of shadow and light that spilled across the grass between the giant trees. She stood in a little column of sunlight herself, her thin blond hair almost transparent in the noon light. Rhonda was silent but now she appeared terribly fragile to Birdie. Her pale eyes squinted in the white heart face, and it almost seemed as if this were the first time the child had stepped out of the half-light of television into the full light of day. The children had forgotten about the squirrels now and were playing a game where they would run from shadow to light, the tree shadows being the safe zones and the full light being the danger zones. They were trying to make it to an empty fountain where there was a statue of a naked boy in the center. "Touch the butt and you win" seemed to be the rule of the game. Rhonda stood perfectly still, watching the little bodies rush in and out of the light and shadow.

"They have their shoes and socks off," she said solemnly.

"Yeah," said Birdie. "The grass feels good under your toes—cool and green. Want to try it?"

"But there might be dog doo or broken glass."

"No. I don't see any. It's safe. Go on." Rhonda didn't move. "Come on, I'll take mine off, too." Birdie slipped off her sandals.

Rhonda looked down at Birdie's bare toes and giggled softly. "You have funny-looking feet."

"Thanks a bunch."

"They're not as funny looking as your eyebrows, though."

"Come on, take your shoes off. It feels great."

Rhonda bent down, unbuckled her Minnie Mouse sandals and stepped out of them. She wiggled her toes in the grass. "It feels funny." Just then the children whizzed by and grazed her shoulder.

"Hey," Birdie said to Rhonda, "you better move quick to a shadow or you'll get caught."

Rhonda ran toward the shade of a giant tupelo tree between her and the fountain. Two other girls pranced around the edge of the shadow. They were a little bit older than Rhonda— maybe five or six—and seemed to take a motherly interest in her. Birdie watched.

"Come on," one said. "We'll help you get to the fountain." They each took one of Rhonda's hands. "One, two, three—go!" they shouted, and all three fled from the deep, cool shade of the tupelo. Their sundresses flew. Six skinny legs, four of them tanned and scraped with summer daring and two pale as milk, skimmed across the grass. The three children clambered over the edge of the fountain into the empty well.

"Touch-a-butt! Home free!" The cries went up as they slapped the bronze backside of the statue.

Rhonda and the three children played a long time. They reminded Birdie of hummingbirds she'd seen in a science film darting about, in and out of the shade and sun. Rhonda's silvery blond hair spun around her like a nimbus of pale light. The white face was flushed, her eyes shiny and quick. She became quite good at the game, almost uncatchable. When the children grew tired of the game, the other girls started to turn cartwheels. Rhonda crouched down to observe them, trying to figure out how they did it. She tried once but crumpled into an all-fours-on-the-ground position. "How do they do that and keep standing?" she asked.

"Look here. I'll demonstrate," Birdie said. "It goes step-hand-hand-step." Birdie reeled through the air. A few more tries and Rhonda had it. Birdie sat down and watched her. She looked like a little silver pinwheel spinning off across the lawn. For the first time ever Birdie thought her niece was pretty. Pretty and smart.

Then they went to the swan boats. They had four rides altogether.

"What do they call these funny trees with the long green leaves?" Rhonda asked as they approached the south end of the pond.

"Weeping willows, because you see how the branches are all long and droopy and sweep the water. It's like the tree is

50

crying." The branches from one tree swept out from the bank so far that a tunnel was created through which the swan boat could pass.

"It's like a weeping tunnel," Rhonda whispered as they glided through the green arch on their giant swan's back. Birdie gave the small, white hand a squeeze.

They had only been home a few minutes. Birdie was in her room reviewing her Filene's orientation book, and Rhonda, still excited about her first real-life experience, had been "yapping" so much about it that Joe couldn't hear the baseball game, so she was sent into the kitchen to yap to Marge and Lainie. There was a sharp rap on Birdie's door.

"Yeah?"

"It's me, Lainie. I want to talk to you about something." The anger in her voice was unmistakable.

"Come in."

The door flew open and Lainie's face was blotchy with rage. Lainie had an unbelievably horrible temper. Rhonda stood cowering behind her. Birdie could not imagine what the cause of all this was. Hadn't she lent Lainie her calculator, hidden her Carol Beth cosmetics kit, taken her kid to the Public Gardens?

"What's eating you?" Birdie said.

"What's eating me?" Lainie raged. "I'll tell you what's eating me! What's this Rhonda tells me about going to the gardens and playing some tag game with a statue where they go and touch his thing?"

"It wasn't his thing, Mommy," Rhonda screamed. "It was his butt. I just saw his thing."

51

"It's all the same."

Now Birdie was furious. "For pete's sake, it's not all the same. A butt's different from a penis, first of all. And secondly, it was a *statue*, not a live person. And thirdly, it was a game of tag, nothing else. And fourthly, it is the first time this kid has ever had any fun away from a TV set."

"It's filthy," hissed Lainie.

"It is not," Rhonda and Birdie both blurted out. "And fifth," Birdie continued, "it's parents who make things filthy for children, not the children."

"Birdie!" Marge Flynn stood in the doorway. "I can't believe what comes out of your mouth these days."

"Comes out of *my* mouth," Birdie nearly shrieked, but Marge was looking worriedly at Lainie, who was bristling like an angry cat.

"Now," Marge said, turning back to Birdie, "wasn't the statue wearing a leaf or something? They always used to."

Birdie rolled her eyes in disbelief. "I don't know. I'm not in the habit of examining every statue in the Public Gardens. When were you there, Ma?"

Even Lainie seemed interested in this. Marge made a curious gesture, something mysteriously young seeming. "Oh, your father and I used to go walking in the gardens before we were married."

Birdie was mesmerized. She wanted to hear more. But Marge was moving away, back from the door, saying, "Birdie's right, Lainie. Rhonda had a lovely afternoon. She met some nice little girls. She went to see the swan boats, didn't you?" Marge looked down but Rhonda was gone.

"Where'd she go?"

52

"It's time for 'Gilligan's Island,' " Lainie said. "I'll take her home to watch." And she swept out of the room, swishing her dignity behind her like the limp train of an evening gown.

Birdie had no taste for dinner that night and went out early to find Timmy. The air was thick with the sweet fragrance of marijuana. There were kids on almost every corner celebrating the end of school, sharing a beer and smoking. It was just getting dark when Birdie started down a small alley on a shortcut to the piers. She was less than a quarter of the way down the alley when she stopped suddenly. Her breath locked in her throat at the sight directly ahead of her—the sight of the bright purple, sandaled feet braced against the car door frame while the knees rocked back and forth in an unmistakable grinding motion. Five or six boys were lined up waiting their turns. The boys were calling out softly, the car creaked rhythmically and a sweet, gasping sound came from Phyllis "Fill 'er up" Dougherty.

"Finish it off!" a voice from the end of the line urged.

"Almost! Almost!"

The car, the line of boys—they all swayed to a rhythm, and Birdie had a sudden vivid image of the tide with its mindless swelling motion. Birdie clamped her mouth shut and pressed her hand to her lips as she began to gag. She knew she was going to vomit in another two seconds and turned to run. Timmy was next.

CHAPTER
7

I can't write. I am writing, because I can't talk about it, but now I can't write, either. I can't think about it, but I do. In other words, I can't stop thinking about it, and if I think about it without doing something I'll throw up again. I think . . . I throw up. That's it since last night. So, Dear Diary, I am writing, just making little marks now on the page to keep me from going crazy. To keep me from throwing up. I shall never, ever, never, never get over this. I don't understand Phyllis. I don't even want to try to understand Phyllis. But there is one thing that I know. I am as mad at Phyllis as I am at that whole line of boys waiting their turn. She has made me feel as scummy as she is. It's like the poem in Heming-

way's book, the one he didn't write—poem, that is. The "No Man Is an Island" one by John Donne.

Birdie got up and found the book. She opened it to the fly leaf and read the poem. Then, with grim defiance, she seized her pen and began to write:

No woman is an island, intire of itselfe. Every woman is a piece of the continent, a part of the Maine. If one woman is . . . .

What word of all the ones described that physical act done without feeling or even lust? Donne's words—"washed away"—weren't all that bad, she thought. The "away" part was good. It meant vanished here, obliterated, erased of an identity. Birdie continued writing:

If any woman is screwed away by the man-tide, I am lesse as well as if Phyllis were, as well as if a manner of thy sister or of thine own were. Any woman's submission diminishes me, because I am involved in womankinde. And therefore, never send to know for whom the bell tolls. It tolls for thee.

Absolutely the worst thing she had ever written. She knew it, but she felt better. Did this mean she was about to become a radical feminist? No, she thought, just a radical human. She had already plotted out her breakfast routine this morning, which was based on seeing as little as possible of Timmy. She didn't feel like eating a lot because her stomach wasn't back to normal and she wondered if it ever would be. As she walked out of her bedroom she braced herself for meeting Timmy. He looked up and started to speak but never articulated one word. Birdie had planned to ask how Phyllis was, but she simply looked at him. There was no need to say anything. The expression on her face was enough. Timmy knew immediately what she had seen.

"I . . . I can explain," Timmy whispered hoarsely.

"Never!"

"Birdie"—her mother turned from the stove—"what do you want for breakfast?"

"Nothing. I've got to get to work early," she said, still looking straight at Timmy. Her eyes bored into him like twin drill bits.

Marge seemed oblivious to the drama going on between her two children. "Nothing? How can you sell on an empty stomach? You need something—coffee, a doughnut at least."

"I'll pick something up on the way."

"Don't you want this jelly roll here? Take this with you to eat on the subway."

"No, Ma. Nothing. Please!"

She picked up her shoulder bag and flew out the door. Nothing from them, from any of them! Her whole rotten family could go to hell. "You, too, lady!" she hissed at the chipped madonna as she stomped past her. There had to be somebody, something for her, something between the madonna and Phyllis Dougherty. And it wasn't her mother.

"I think this divided skirt is very slenderizing. Don't you, Jane?" The immense woman, her red hair lacquered into rigid submission, was speaking to her equally large friend. Birdie nodded along with Jane and thought, Yes, if you divide by two, the skirt could be considered "slenderizing." It was an interesting word—slenderizing. It made one feel thin just saying it. This was the third customer in forty-five minutes to use the word. Since the store had opened almost an hour and a half ago, Birdie had sold nearly one thousand dollars' worth of clothes. She had put on the "happy face that sells" that she had learned about in training sessions and within a short time had stuffed women into jogging outfits, divided skirts and assorted pants suits. Selling, although not an antidote to the horrible scene of the night before, was something of a diversion. She could not think about it. The vile image, those bright purple, sandaled feet braced against the car door, receded somewhat, although not entirely, to the back of her brain while she sold.

At 11:30 she went on break. Gloria's break was earlier, and since Birdie didn't know anyone else to have coffee with, she decided to go up to the Collection Shop where the most expensive clothes of all were sold and just have herself a look around. There was no one above a size ten when she stepped off the elevator on the fourth floor. There were no racks, either, only islands with mannequins and designer clothes. Scattered between the islands were a few elegant chairs upholstered in gray velvet. There was a woman on one chair. She was blonde and lanky. She wore a white summer suit. Her long, tanned legs were extended and crossed casually at the ankles. She stretched and ran her fingers through her hair, which was loosely pulled back. "Miss Kaye, can you bring out the Yves Saint Laurent again?" Cripes, Birdie thought. The woman shimmered before her like a mirage. Birdie made her way toward designer sportswear at the other end of the floor and began to look through the Ralph Lauren prairie skirts. In another three weeks, the unsold ones would be heading for the basement. She would try one on now so she would know what to get when they dropped five floors. The eight was too tight around the waist but the ten was perfect. The blouse shown with it was ninety dollars. Forget it. She and Gloria could find something in the basement for ten.

Within fifteen minutes Birdie was back in the basement, selling. She still had on the happy face, but images from the night before kept pushing their way into her mind. She tried to focus on the cool, blond woman in the white suit she had seen in the Collections Shop. It was difficult. Purple-sandaled feet kept breaking through. She had another forty-five minutes until her lunch break at 1:30 with Gloria. The choice was either to eat very early or very late, due to the lunchtime rush when people flooded into the basement.

"Ready?" Gloria looked trim in her navy linen jacket and tan skirt with inverted pleats.

"Just a second." Birdie rang out her register and showed her replacement, an elderly lady who usually worked in better handbags, where the odd-sized jogging suits were on the rack, and the slightly damaged divided skirts. "Those divided skirts are the pits," she whispered to Gloria as she put on her maroon linen jacket, identical to Gloria's except for size and color. "I wouldn't be caught dead in one. A size four came in here this morning and tried one on. She looked like a fourteen in it!"

"Listen," Gloria said as they went by the running shoe

center. "You don't know what big is until you've worked in Big Lady lingerie. Bras the size of pup tents. I feel like I'm working in Eastern Mountain Sports. What do you want for lunch? The usual?"

"Yeah. There's a yogurt place right on the corner. What are you having?"

"My mom packed me some cold pizza." Gloria patted her shoulder bag. "All I need is a Coke."

"Okay. We can get that here and then eat on the mall."

They cut across the basement to the Washington Street exit. Just before the stairs was a hot dog stand across from the moderate-priced shoes. There were tables with every kind of shoe imaginable. On top of one pile—glaring like purple beacons—were sandals identical to Phyllis Dougherty's. The greasy smells from the hot dog stand assaulted Birdie, and she felt she might be sick right there. She bit her lip and prayed to God not to let her throw up in Filene's. She grabbed Gloria's elbow. "When we get to the mall I've got to tell you something really sickening." Gloria's pale gray eyes under the straight, dark brows widened.

"What is it?"

"Wait."

"You look funny."

"There's nothing funny about it." Birdie crossed her eyes slightly, which was a way she had of indicating despair and disbelief. Gloria knew the signal.

"Okay," said Gloria.

Birdie felt better once they were up in the fresh air. She had even taken one bite of her boysenberry yogurt.

"Can you tell me now?" Gloria asked.

"Last night . . . ." Birdie began. Ten minutes later she had told her the whole story of what she had seen in the alley.

"It's absolutely the grossest thing I've ever heard!" Gloria said when Birdie finally finished.

"I know. I never thought I'd tell you, but I just had to. It's like I just couldn't live with it alone, by myself."

"I know what you mean."

"You do?" Birdie asked with relief. "I mean, it's so nauseating I didn't want to make you sick, too."

"I won't be sick. You saw it, after all—that's the worst. I've only heard it." Gloria shook her head fiercely as if trying to dispel the last fragments of any image she might have had. The mass of tight curls that framed her face trembled as if in sympathy.

"What am I suppose to do now?" Birdie sighed.

"Do?" Gloria nearly shouted the word. "There's nothing you can do. What do you mean?"

"Well, I have to live with Timmy, you know. The sight of him makes me want to barf."

"He certainly hasn't been putting in winning performances lately."

"That's an understatement. You know, with the synagogue thing I thought he was wrong. I thought it was horrible. But I also felt he had sort of bottomed out." Birdie thought again of Mrs. Pearlo-what mounting the stairs and seeing the hideous scrawls on the door. "It was as if he had reached his lowest level and had no place to go but up. But this—this is something else. I don't understand it. It's not worse than the synagogue, if you know what I mean. After all, everyone knows what Phyllis is, but it's weird. There's this weird kind of . . . of . . ."—she searched for a word—"violence."

"But no one forced Phyllis to do it. You said so yourself."

"I know. I don't understand it at all. Phyllis did it but it's kind of like it happened to me."

"Birdie," Gloria said and then stopped. "Birdie, you . . . you—"

"I what?"

"You worry me sometimes." Gloria blurted out the words.

"What do you mean, I worry you? I'm not supposed to worry you. I'm supposed to worry my mother."

"Why are you lumping yourself in with Phyllis? You lump yourself in with Phyllis and you lump me in with her, too."

"That's just the point, Gloria!"

"What do you mean, 'that's just the point'? We are nothing, nothing like Phyllis!"

"I know we're nothing like her, but to them . . . ." Birdie struggled.

She was beginning to perceive the glimmerings of a nauseating idea. Birdie looked straight ahead and spoke slowly. "To them, when they were doing that to Phyllis, it didn't matter. It could have been any girl."

"But it was Phyllis, and she was asking for it." Gloria was obviously trying to squeeze enough rationality into her voice to keep herself from exploding in frustration.

"Who even knows if *that's* true? And anyway, it doesn't matter. They shouldn't have done it or wanted to do it."

"But that's the way guys *are*."

"Baloney!" Birdie snapped.

"Well, it's hormones or something."

"I don't believe in hormones."

"What do you mean, you don't believe in hormones, Birdie?" Gloria laughed. "It's not supposed to be a religion. It's a fact—a medical fact."

"Well, do you believe that idiot doctor who said women couldn't be president because they get periods and have raging hormonal imbalances, which would make them blow up the world? I mean, did Harry Truman have his period when he dropped the atomic bomb on Hiroshima?"

Gloria stared hard at Birdie. "How did we get from Phyllis to Hiroshima?"

"Hormones."

"Oh!" said Gloria somewhat absently, as if she were trying to link together all the little pieces in this conversation that had brought them this far.

"I mean, hormones or not, Gloria, would you ever want to be with a guy who'd stood in line waiting for his turn with Phyllis?"

"Oh, Birdie!" Gloria said weakly. "I mean, why even imagine it?"

"Well, if you're saying all these guys have hormones, then there's a chance that somewhere, sometime, every man in the world might have stood in that line."

"Well, okay, as long as the guy knows it's me and not Phyllis. It's a medical fact, as they say."

"What? That they have hormones?"

"Yeah. I mean, try finding somebody without them, Birdie."

"Medical facts aren't truth."

"What does that mean?" Gloria asked.

"I'm not sure," Birdie said wearily. But this time she was not thinking about Phyllis or the purple sandals. She was thinking about Mrs. Pearlo-what on the stairs of the synagogue.

CHAPTER 8

Birdie sat very still on a stool in the Saccharellis' kitchen as Gloria's mother wound small sections of her hair around tiny rods. She squirted the sections periodically with a bottle of lotion.

"How much more?" Birdie asked.

"Not much."

"I'm feeling guilty."

"Why should you feel guilty?" Rose Saccharelli asked.

"Because you're wearing swimming goggles and rubber gloves all for me."

"Forget it. My eyes are just sensitive, now that I don't do this as a full-time occupation. So it protects them, but I really like getting back to this occasionally."

"What we need are gas masks," Mr. Saccharelli's voice boomed from an adjacent room.

"See? I feel guilty."

"Don't feel guilty," the voice called in again. "I'm just jealous. I wouldn't mind having hair to curl."

"You should never feel guilty about looking nice, Birdie," Rose Saccharelli said firmly. "Looking good is cheap psychiatric care."

"That's just what our training leader said at Filene's, Mom," said Gloria. "That's the line we're supposed to use when someone's trying on clothes. If they say it feels good or 'I feel great in this but it's too expensive,' you say, 'Think of it as cheap psychotherapy.' "

"Well, they're right, and Birdie is going to look and feel much better now that she has all her hair cut off. It was dragging you down mentally. I can tell these things."

Birdie only wished it was that simple. Mrs. Saccharelli did not know what was really dragging her down, but after their lunch at the mall Gloria had decided that a permanent was the thing Birdie needed "to do." Well, what else could she suggest? A boyfriend? Hardly, given the circumstances. Winning the lottery? A change of scenery? The options were not only limited but virtually nonexistent. Changes in hairstyles, in a sense, meant new beginnings. Short of total escape from her family and East Boston, it was the best she could do. Gloria had become a one-person pep rally. She—Birdie—was going to change her hairstyle. It would be "liberating." They found a copy of the Lauren prairie skirt in the basement. Cheaper and better lines for her. Now all they had to do was to sell their way out of the basement. By Christmas time, Gloria

65

predicted, they should be on the third floor in better dresses, by spring the hallowed realm of the fourth floor—designer clothes! Another year or so and they could enter the buyer training program. The small, stylish apartment with brick walls, wicker and plants could not be that far off—someplace between the fourth floor and the buyer training program.

Birdie had to admit that she was feeling better. She always did when she was at the Saccharellis'.

"What are you reading now, Mrs. Saccharelli?"

Rose Saccharelli took a pick out of her mouth and stuck it through the last rod she had placed at the nape of Birdie's neck. "*Passion's Nectar*. Get me that hair net, will you, Gloria? It's a Louise Sheridan. I don't like it as much as her others. It's set in New Mexico on a ranch. All that sand and cactus. Ech!"

"Rose likes the New York penthouse-limo scene." Vinnie Saccharelli had walked into the kitchen and patted his wife's backside. "Rural settings are not Rosie's cup of tea. Right?" He chuckled.

"That's not true, Vinnie," Rose said, removing the swimming goggles. "I loved that one, *Island's Heat*, and that was Honolulu."

"I've never been there, but I don't think it's all that rural, Mom."

"It's an island."

"So's East Boston." Vinnie laughed.

Forty-five minutes later, Rose Saccharelli began running her fingers through Birdie's hair as she sat under the heat lamps.

66

"It's gorgeous. Your hair took it beautifully. Look at this, Gloria! Soft, lovely curls. You've got beautiful hair, Birdie. So rich and dark with your blue eyes!"

Birdie walked out into the summer night. The light cap of curls felt soft and glistening. She could imagine beams of starlight caught in the ringlets. She felt renewed and strengthened. Permanents are better than confession, she thought briefly. Not that she had ever taken confession too seriously. There had been a time she could hardly remember now, when church had really excited her. But her enthusiasm started to dwindle just about the time of her confirmation. She was eleven or twelve and, like all prospective confirmees, was expected to choose a confirmation name. At the time pink was her favorite color, and she thought it would be great to be named Pinky. The sisters thought otherwise. So it became Rose instead, an obscure connection with the Saccharellis. Birdie had felt shortchanged. No, not shortchanged, she thought to herself, more like short-circuited in the process, and it was then that the decline of her enthusiasm for the church had begun. Religion shouldn't do that to you, not in her book, short out on you like that. The breeze off the harbor felt nice, and she was enjoying walking alone and being quiet with her less-than-shimmering thoughts under her shining cap of new curls. So what if there hadn't been a Saint Pinky! Would it have killed them to let her call herself Pinky or even Pinky Rose? She would have outgrown it in a couple of years. It wasn't like it was any big deal. After all: "What's in a name? That which we call a rose/By any other name would smell as sweet. . . ."

She remembered having to memorize that one last year when they were reading *Romeo and Juliet* in Mr. Jenner's class. The passage appeared on the final in the fill-in-the-blank section of the exam: "A _____ by any other _____ would smell as _____." Not too imaginative, Mr. Jenner. She thought about those blanks, and the church, for which obedience, not personal aspiration, was the name of the game. But she wasn't a blank to be filled in by the church. That might work for her mom, and it had worked for her when she was very small, being a very good and obedient small child dressed like a miniature bride in her size four first communion dress.

The blank, as far as Birdie saw it, was not herself, but between herself and the church. It was not just a blank. She felt a new metaphor lurking around the rim of her brain. If one thought of the church as a connection point between oneself and God, then something had shorted out. Electricity was hardly her field, but on this warm, starcast July night, why not search for a new metaphor? So then, if something had shorted out, in all honesty did that Great Transformer in the Sky really give two hoots if at the age of eleven she wanted to be called Pinky? Birdie pushed her hands down into her jean pockets and walked on more briskly now.

She was at the piers. She had been so absorbed in her little philosophical discourses that she had not been aware of taking this route. The moon just rising beat a silver path across the water right to the end of the pier where she saw him. There was no mistaking. She turned and began walking to where the silvered water met the pilings, to the solitary figure at the end.

"Why'd you do that with Phyllis Dougherty?"

Timmy, his head turned slightly to the left, continued to look straight across the water toward the east, toward the sea entrance to the harbor.

"I didn't do it," he said quietly, and before Birdie could ask another question, he added in an almost toneless voice, "I couldn't do it."

"You mean, you decided not to?" Birdie asked cautiously.

"No!" Timmy said abruptly. "I couldn't. I wasn't able to do it. Get it?" He turned slowly toward his sister for the first time. "And it's not the first time I couldn't, either. The first time was last month, the night of"—he paused—"the prank."

Birdie was taken aback. "What do you mean, unable? I thought guys could always do it." Immediately, Birdie knew that she had said precisely the wrong thing.

"Not this guy, Birdie!" Timmy almost shouted.

"Timmy!" His face was twisted and white and ugly. Tears coursed down his cheeks. Birdie had grabbed his arm and was holding it tight.

He wrenched free. "Don't worry. I won't jump in. I'd probably botch up drowning, too."

"Timmy, don't talk like that."

"What do you care?"

"I don't really know." And at that moment within her she felt both revulsion and concern, love and anger. It was a stupefying blend of emotions, but she spoke about the one emotion she did not feel.

"I don't feel sorry for you, Timmy. I might care, but I sure don't feel sorry for you."

"I didn't ask you to." He turned his head away and looked

69

out across the water, toward the east again, as if searching for an early dawn. Birdie looked across the harbor at the buildings that made the twinkling skyline of Boston. She knew that the residents of those buildings were not always merry, sitting around in designer jeans sipping Kahlua and cream, but it sure beat sitting on the end of a pier in East Boston with a totally messed-up brother from a complete wreck of a family.

Birdie wasn't sure why she stayed sitting there, but she did. The water, she guessed, gave her a sense of connection to other things, and on a calm, clear night it was lighter near the water with its reflections of moon and stars and lighted buildings than it was on a city street. Timmy, she knew, felt the same way about the water. You needed to feel connected to other things, at times, and you needed to feel the light during the nighttime, too. It was a legitimate need, almost a physiological one, Birdie thought.

"What'd you do to your hair?"

"Cut it and had a permanent. Gloria's mom did it."

"It looks okay."

Birdie didn't respond. She could hear the music from the jazz boat cruising across the harbor. The boat had just pulled away from its pier and was beginning its circuit. Four evenings a week during the summer months the music boats left Long Wharf for their cruises of the harbor. One evening was jazz, one blues, one country and western, and one evening classical. In about forty-five minutes the boat would be near where Timmy and Birdie sat. They would be able to hear all

70

the life on the boat quite clearly, the music, and, if it were between sets, the timballing sound of glasses and ice cubes, the talk and the laughter that swirled up through the night.

"That night . . ." Timmy began suddenly. "Not the night with Phyllis. The other night." His voice lowered to a husky whisper. "The night of . . . when we went to the synagogue . . . ."

Would they ever sit on the end of this pier and talk about anything good and positive? Birdie wondered. "Yes," she said in response to Timmy. Her eyes fastened on the winking lights of the music boat.

"You know, I really didn't do that much. I told you mine were just scrawls and stuff. Mostly I just watched them do it."

"Timmy!" Birdie sighed with disgust.

"It's the truth, Birdie. I didn't do anything! I just watched them."

"Well, why did you watch?"

"I had to. I mean, what was I supposed to do?"

"Stop them!"

Timmy's eyes opened wide. "What are you talking about? Are you crazy? How do you stop them?"

"You tell them that they're a bunch of creeps. You tell them that only morons would take time to do something like this! Would *think* of doing something like this. You tell them that only cowards and weak-minded turds would get their kicks from vandalizing something that has value and meaning for somebody else, that only idiots whose lives have no value and no meaning themselves would do it." There was a long pause.

Birdie was breathing hard. "And one more thing, Timmy. It's not true you didn't do anything. Even if you hadn't made a squiggle, you did do something. You watched and said nothing. You let it happen."

They sat for a long time now. The black sky clouded up, obscuring the moon, and the night grew darker. The buildings across the harbor lost their definition and seemed like disembodied aggregates of small lights arranged in strips and blocks. The music boat had passed by again. Its passengers had disembarked at Long Wharf, and a new group had boarded for a late-night cruise.

"Wind switched around," Timmy said.

"Yeah. Feels wet."

"Coming from the southeast."

"Probably going to be a lousy day tomorrow," Birdie said as if she had no stake in that day, anyway.

"Are you working?" Timmy asked.

"No, I got the day off. How 'bout you?"

"Half day off." Timmy paused. "I got an interview."

"An interview? What for?" Birdie asked.

"Job over there." Timmy nodded to the lights across the black water.

"What? What? What is it?" Birdie was excited.

"It's nothing."

"You always talk in negatives."

"Well, it's a dishwashing job," Timmy said abruptly. "Does that sound more positive?"

"Where?"

"Old Ironsides."

"The restaurant in Quincey Market?" Birdie's eyes brightened.

"That's it. Not the one tied up at the pier in Charlestown."

"Very funny. When do you start?"

"I haven't had the interview yet, Birdie."

"You'll get the job."

"Maybe."

"And then you can work your way up to something better."

"Maybe."

It's a start, Birdie wrote in her diary later that night. Inside the apartment the rest of the family slept, but Birdie sat out on the fire escape. The moon had gone. The music cruises were finished. Her eyes were so accustomed now to the darkness that she could discern the outlines of the buildings. The lights no longer appeared suspended in the darkness, but part of a structure.

We'll be part of it, too [she wrote]. *This is a start for Timmy, away from all this to something. There's bound to be someone better than Benny Arlette over there. I'm still mad at Timmy but when I sit up here in the soft darkness of this night and I see those little pulses of light across the water, well, I want him to at least . . . .*

At least what? Birdie stopped writing. She chewed briefly on the end of her pen and watched a tugboat come in. Its bright red and green lights punctuated the graying light as night melted into dawn. The view from where she sat was nice, she thought, especially at this early hour of the morning. There was a clarity of vision, and everything seemed to be in some sort of brief repose, except, of course, for the little tugboat that went its way down the middle of the harbor with a feisty singleness of purpose.

CHAPTER

"Not a cannon in sight!" Birdie muttered. They don't need a dishwasher, she thought, they need a historian.

"What is this place, Aunt Birdie?" Rhonda asked.

"It's a restaurant. Timmy's working here."

They had just walked through the double glass doors and were standing in an entryway that had been designed to resemble the afterdeck of a sailing ship with wide plank floors, swags of rope and brass fixtures. Beyond the entryway it looked pretty much like the typical "New Boston" restaurant done in an old Boston building. There were the exposed brick walls, the numerous hanging plants. Despite a few blown-up photographs showing the old battleship's rigging that suggested a slightly nautical atmosphere, it didn't look any more like the *Constitution* than a taxicab did. A man in an impeccably tailored suit approached them. No double knits here, Birdie thought. He bowed slightly in a gesture that seemed to Birdie more condescending than welcoming in its nature.

"Luncheon is not served until twelve."

"We don't want lunch. We're here to see my brother, Tim Flynn. He works in the kitchen."

"Oh, yes. He should be going on break now. I'll tell him you're here." He turned to leave.

"What's luncheon, Aunt Birdie?"

"Lunch with an 'un' on the end."

Timmy came through some swinging doors in the back of the restaurant.

"I knew you couldn't stay away." He laughed.

"Want to have an early lunch with Rhonda and me? We're on our way to the library."

"I want to go to that hot dog place," Rhonda said.

"Well, you couldn't afford anything here," Timmy answered. "Okay. Let's go. I only have twenty minutes. Then I have to be back for the lunch crowd."

"Don't fall in, Rhonda. I don't want to have to fish you out," Timmy said.

"I won't."

They were sitting on the end of India Wharf with their feet hanging over the edge while they ate their hot dogs. Birdie ate a frozen yogurt. She would have preferred to be sitting in the middle of the marketplace on a bench watching the strolling minstrels, the people and the vendors, but Timmy had announced that after three days of working in Boston's busiest tourist attraction he had overdosed on the market. "One more of those pantomime creeps and I puke," he said. So now they were at the end of one pier looking across the water toward the pier where they had been sitting just the night before.

There was no skyline over there, Birdie thought. Just low, shabby buildings. The Bethlehem Steel shipyard added nothing to the scene except a few cranes. These and the continual landings and takeoffs of jets from the airport that sprawled into the harbor were the only punctuation points in the sky above East Boston. The irony of the scene suddenly struck Birdie: People paid tremendous rent for harbor-view apartments on this side, but to look across was ugly. The good view was from the other side, East Boston, where she lived. But maybe if you were a part of the view, you didn't need one to look at. She would rather be a part of it than not; to be in it rather than looking at it.

"What a mess," she said out loud.

Timmy's head was turned to the right. He was looking out the harbor mouth, to sea. "Yeah," he answered softly, not even turning his head. Yet he seemed to know what she was talking about. "But it used to be *the* place, Bird."

"When was that—the cave days?"

"No. The clipper days. Right over there"—Timmy pointed to the left of the Bethlehem yards—"were the McKay yards. Fastest sailing ships ever built came from right there."

"No more," said Birdie. "We've got jets, not clippers."

Birdie and Rhonda got off the subway at Copley Square and walked through the entrance to the new wing of the library. There were some display tables in the lobby with books and some posters on the wall. A man with a gaunt face and hollow eyes stared out from a poster into the marble lobby. Birdie looked quickly, then again. Was it a corpse that stared out so intently? Rhonda pulled her hand. Out of the corner of her eye she caught a fragment of another poster. These eyes were alive and disbelieving, and they were the eyes of a child.

"C'mon, Aunt Birdie, you said there's a children's room here." Birdie walked away quickly. "Turn here," she said. They were in a carpeted room, full of sunlight. There were low tables with child-sized chairs. Stands held brightly illustrated picture books. A young librarian came up to them. "Story Circle is about to begin. Would you like to join?" she asked, bending over to Rhonda.

"No."

"What do you mean, Rhonda? How often do you get to go to a story time? Come on."

"I want my library card. You said we could get one—free." She looked directly at the librarian.

"Okay. We'll get your card first," the librarian said. "Follow me."

Five minutes later—clutching her temporary borrower's card—Rhonda joined the group. Birdie sat with her for a few minutes and listened to the story. It was something about a bunch of little fish that were frightened by a big fish and how they decided to all swim together so they would look like one gigantic fish. Rhonda seemed quite enthralled, so Birdie whispered in her ear that she would be back in a minute.

The man in the poster was alive. That was perhaps the worst part of it, that he had lived to stare out with his horror-swept eyes forever. He seemed to Birdie the possessor of some terrible secret. Birdie moved slowly through the exhibit. She had heard about the Holocaust. They had read about it in school. She had even seen a picture once of corpses from the camps, piled up like kindling. But there was one photograph in this exhibit that she kept coming back to. It was not that of the man with the terrible secret, nor the one of the bodies piled atop one another. It was a different picture, the one she had caught a glimpse of on her way in with Rhonda. It was a picture of a small boy. He was eight or nine years old and he was standing on a station platform. The eyes were not swept with horror, but disbelief—disbelief that something was about to happen and that nothing would ever be the same again. Birdie looked at that picture and then hurried back to the children's room. The first time, she went to see if Rhonda was still in the story circle. She was. A new story had been started, and another librarian was setting out art materials for some sort of crafts project. She returned to the lobby to look at the boy in the picture again. Then she went back a second time to the children's room. The Mother Goose mobile made of bright, cutout shapes moved slowly in a column of sunlight. The children were still listening, so once more she went back and looked at the small boy with his disbelieving eyes. Over the posters were words printed in large display letters on Lucite panels. Birdie began to read them now:

Never shall I forget that night, the first night in camp, which has turned my life into one long night, . . . Never shall I forget that smoke. Never shall I forget the little faces of the children, whose bodies I saw turned into wreaths of smoke beneath a silent, blue sky.

A kind of horrific panic seized Birdie. She rushed back to the children's room. The Mother Goose mobile still turned in the shaft of sunlight. The story circle had broken. The children were now in a new circle cutting out fish shapes. Rhonda was busily at work, part of the circle. Birdie was drawn back to the lobby. It had become a magnetic field. She read on:

Never shall I forget those flames, which consumed my faith forever.

At the end of the quotation was a name—Elie Weisel. There was one word after the name—survivor. She read that one horrifying grouping of words again. ". . . the children, whose bodies I saw turned into wreaths of smoke beneath a silent, blue sky." This time Birdie walked slowly back to the children's room. The distance was a short one. There was no corridor between the lobby and the children's room. The space between the two flowed together in an easy continuity. Yet things had become strangely discontinuous for Birdie. How could these two orders of things exist? How could she be looking at a record of something unthinkable in its horror one moment and the next moment be standing in a room splashed with sunlight, nursery rhyme mobiles and tiny children proudly holding bright cutouts of fish?

Birdie winced at the impeccable blueness of the sky that was clear and flawless overhead on their brief walk between the library and the descending stairs for the subway. Under her arm she held several books; with her other hand she clutched Rhonda's. She began reading on the trip home. The book was slim—167 pages long. It was as if a scream had been pressed between its covers, one long, agonizing scream. " 'I can't do that,' a small boy said when ordered by an SS guard to tie the noose around his father's neck. But he finally did it. His father begged him to."

"Can I eat my candy now, Aunt Birdie?"

"Sure."

"But let go of my hand. I can't eat when you're holding it, silly."

"Oh." She tried to look interested in the candy Rhonda was unwrapping. "Is it peppermint or cinnamon?"

"Cherry," Rhonda answered and popped the ball into her mouth. There was something so ungraspable about everything now. Birdie wondered if things would ever seem sensible again. The subway hurtled along. They changed at Park Street and again at Government Center.

"What are you reading, Aunt Birdie?"

"A book."

"I know, silly. What's it about?"

"Oh, you wouldn't understand."

"I understand more than you think."

Birdie felt her stomach clench a little. She swallowed hard. The pale, little heart-shaped face looked up at her, waiting for an explanation.

"Why don't you just look out the window, Rhonda?"

"It's black. There's nothing to see, silly."

CHAPTER
10

She felt removed, as if she were enveloped in some sort of fog and the rest of the family sat in clear morning light. But it was evening. She had been reading the books all afternoon, and the only light was the television's bright colors.

"What a student!" Marge said, looking up from her game of solitaire. "You must be starved. Reading right through dinner. Food for thought is one thing, but you're still a growing girl."

"Your mother's right, Birdie. I don't want you looking like no Gloria. That's too skinny. So is that what's her name you're always talking about—Chicago Wells."

"Paris Wells, Grandpa!" Rhonda, over again with Lainie, turned from the television. "And I want a Paris Wells doll.

She comes with a complete wardrobe and her own miniature hairdryer and sports car.''

Once again Birdie was struck by the discontinuity. She had walked out of her bedroom, where, for the afternoon, time had ceased to be as she read about the most inconceivable events. And now she was standing in the living room, caught in the swamp of the television's candy light. She wasn't imagining it, but the mood seemed unusually light. Her father wasn't yelling and her mother wasn't nervously chain-smoking. Birdie stood and looked at the family. They really did seem more relaxed, but there was something odd: Nobody was talking, either. Joe read his newspaper, Lainie stared out the window and Marge played solitaire. They were all solitaire players, Birdie thought and suddenly realized that without Timmy there was no reason for anyone to talk with anyone else. No one to argue with, yell at or pray for. There was a queer stillness in the room. The people seemed strangely hollow. They need Timmy, she thought. We need Timmy. That's what makes us work as a family. It was odd. Then she thought of those families standing in squares of European towns with names she had never heard, or on train platforms, and of the children—the lucky ones—who saw their parents disappear forever as the SS troops slammed them into trains, or later, if the children had not escaped the trains, at the camps where families newly arrived were directed either to the right or the left. The elderly, the mothers with young children, inevitably to the left, the side of death. And here they were, the Flynns, together, whole and yet with this stillness at their center. She had started to speak, but her mouth was so dry she first had to swallow and her voice in its initial sound was slightly raw.

"What were you doing in 1942?"

"Huh?" Marge looked up just as she was about to place the queen of spades.

"I said, what were you doing in 1942?"

"Well, that's certainly a funny question. I was only two years old. You expect me to remember? Let's see, if it was summer I was probably at Revere Beach; winter. . . ." Her voice trailed off.

"You were only two?" Birdie said, somewhat disappointed.

"Sure, what did you think I was, a teenager? If I had been, I'd be almost sixty now, for goodness sakes!"

"Do you remember anything about the war?" Birdie persisted.

"No. Not really."

"I remember," Joe said, putting down the paper. "We had a victory garden just down the street toward the runways with the Santinis, which was great, 'cause you know Italians are fabulous gardeners. And then Joey Santini and I used to go down by the piers at low tide, right underneath them, and collect scrap metal. They called us the Joe Boy Team." Joe's eyes warmed with the memory. "We were just about ten or eleven years old, but we brought in almost half a ton of metal between July 1942 and March '43. More than Father Feliciano's group, the Boy Scouts or the Cubs. Just the two of us! And then you know what else I remember?" Joe said, lifting his finger. His face had a sudden animation. "There was this old geezer. McCardle was his name. He worked over in the Customs House Tower and he was convinced that there were U-boats coming into Boston Harbor. Of course, nobody paid any attention to him except Joey and me, but pretty soon he had us convinced. So Joey and me used to sneak out at night to go on U-boat patrol down by the water, and we rigged up this thing on the roof of Joey's house with tin pans and flashlights, and if we saw one we were going to send signals. You know, like the 'one if by land, two if by sea' bit. Of course, this would be two.''

"Who were you going to flash them to?" Birdie asked.

"To McCardle. He worked three or four nights a week over at the tower. It was a lot of fun until Mrs. Santini started wondering where all her tin stuff was going, and then the old man found us on the roof. Phew! What a licking we got!''

"Was that it?" Birdie asked.

"Was what it?" Joe looked at her somewhat puzzled.

"The war."

"Well, that's all I can remember, except it was, in a funny way, a good time—everybody pulling together. Our garden with the Santinis was beautiful. I remember your grandma, God rest her. She and Mrs. Santini planted marigolds between the tomato plants to keep the bugs off them. That was Mrs. Santini's idea. It worked. Smart, them Wops.'' Joe chuckled warmly. "The orange flowers and the red tomatoes! Still my favorite colors, you know.''

"But what about Hitler and the concentration camps and all those people dying in ovens?"

"Birdie, watch it!" Marge shot her a glance. "Little people have big ears.'' She nodded toward Rhonda.

"Nobody knew a damn thing about that, Birdie, until the war was over. That was '45.'' Joe had picked up his paper again.

"So what did you think when you heard about it? You were older then. What did people do?"

"Do? There wasn't nothing to do. It had been done. And you know what? No offense now to nobody." Joe folded his paper carefully and laid it across his knee. Birdie felt a warm queasiness welling up in the back of her throat. What was he going to say? What in God's name was he going to say?

"Dad, you want a beer? I'm getting one," Lainie said, uncurling herself from the sofa.

"Sure, sweetie. As I was saying"—Birdie wasn't sure she wanted to hear—"with no offense, and I don't believe it didn't happen, mind you, but I think it was greatly exaggerated."

"But, Dad!" Birdie was flabbergasted.

"Don't 'but, Dad' me," Joe said evenly, without temper. Just don't let him call me "missy," Birdie thought. "I'm just saying that there were some concentration camps and reportedly a number of Jews were killed, but . . . ."

"What do you mean, 'reportedly a number,' Dad? Six million people were killed and there are survivors to tell it."

"Don't use that tone with your father, Birdie."

"Thank you, Marge. I'm just saying you know how newspapers can distort things."

"Well, how come you read them all the time?"

"Okay!" Joe roared. "That's enough lip from you, missy!" There, he'd done it.

Lainie came out of the kitchen with two beers. "I can't believe it," she said, handing Joe his beer. "We're sitting here having a nice family evening and you have to start a fight, Birdie, about something that happened over forty years ago.

I thought I'd come over here, you know, Timmy's out, no chance for a scene, and look who's picking a fight!''

"I'm not picking a fight," Birdie said dully.

"Don't knock Timmy, Lainie. He's been paying me back every week for the lawyer's fee and the fine.''

"You think that's just going to wipe it out, don't you?'' Birdie spoke quietly.

"Now what are you talking about?'' Joe looked over the top of his paper.

"What he did to the synagogue, to those people. You think someone like that lady with the tattoo is ever going to forget coming up those stairs and seeing the swastika?''

"Well, what the hell do you expect us to do, Birdie? I can't undo history. Even if it did happen, what else can I do except pay the goddamn lawyer and Timmy's fine? And what am I suppose to do for this old lady with the tattoo? We weren't involved in that. We were over here—lace-curtain Irish, not Germans!''

"I know," Birdie said softly. But the distance was no help. She could still hear the dead babies crying out and see the wreaths of smoke that were once children.

"Miss Bleeding Heart!'' Lainie sighed.

"Lainie!'' exclaimed Marge. "Birdie is a very sensitive girl. I've even been thinking a lot lately that you should consider being a nun, Birdie—one of the teaching orders.''

"Ma!'' Birdie had to fight for every ounce of control she could muster. "I can't be a nun.''

"Why?'' Marge set the deck down and stroked the top card nervously. She swallowed hard. "You're not pregnant?''

"No, I'm not pregnant!" Then Birdie shouted, "I don't believe in God! That's why!"

The cards fell on the floor as Marge jumped up. But it was her father who was across the room in one swift step. The smack of his hand on Birdie's cheek split the queer stillness of the room.

"You what?" Gloria's voice was slightly incredulous on the other end of the phone.

"I've been grounded." Birdie was speaking low from the phone in the kitchen, but she knew her mom could still hear her.

"Yeah, I heard that the first time. But run the other part by me again—the reason."

Birdie sighed. "Because I don't believe in God."

"Jesus!" exclaimed Gloria.

"That seems to be the problem at the moment."

"Well, what are you going to do?"

"What can I do?"

"Well, are you going to be grounded forever? I mean, until you start believing?"

"When I'm eighteen, there's not much they can do about it."

"That's a long time off, Birdie!"

"I know."

"It might be worthwhile, Birdie, to . . . uh . . . how should I put it . . . ." There was a click on the other end of the phone.

"This is Marge Flynn, Gloria. Now, don't worry about Birdie. We're just having a little family problem." Birdie crossed her eyes slightly as she listened to her mother make a neat, acceptable parcel out of what had been a dreadful family argument that had ended in physical violence.

She had been called missy, slapped, sent to her room and grounded, a quadruple whammy in terms of punishment and humiliation to be meted out by her parents. But she really didn't care anymore. She had no desire to sit around with her family, charming as they were! She was supposed to have gone to Gloria's, but she'd see her tomorrow at work. It had started to rain. She watched the droplets course down her bedroom windowpane. If a bolt of lightning came through the window and struck her teddy bear, would she start believing again? Fat chance. She read on. The rainy night became laced with the long, agonizing screams. Sometimes it actually seemed to hurt to read, and often she felt a nausea building in her stomach. But she kept reading. The horror was never so distilled, so completely revealed, as in the words from the autobiography of Rudolph Hoess, commandant of Auschwitz.

> The gassings were carried out in Block Eleven. Protected by a gas mask, I watched the killing myself . . . a short—almost smothered—cry and it was all over . . . many of the women (on the way to the gas chambers) would hide their children among piles of clothing. The men from the special detachment were on the lookout for this. . . . The smaller children usually cried, but when their mothers or members of the special detachment comforted them, they became calm and entered the gas chamber playing or joking with one another and carrying their toys.

Birdie finally stopped reading after midnight. She was horrified by what she had read. She felt virtually awash in the gruesome descriptions of the crematoriums and gas chambers that worked ceaselessly, day and night, to obliterate a race of people from the earth. She wanted to scream but felt mute. Wouldn't this scream sound shrill and perhaps even phony after the millions of screams that preceded hers? She did not have the language to describe this event to herself. Language would only trivialize it. There was no right speech for the agonies. And in spite of the graphic descriptions, she still could not imagine much of what she had read. Yet she did not doubt a word of it.

It was the silence that woke her. The rain had stopped just before dawn. Perhaps she had never been asleep, for she seemed to remember hearing that last drop of rain and then the quiet, the silence of the rain stopping. If she had slept, it had only been two hours at the most. She put on her bathrobe, walked from her bedroom through the living room and crawled out the window onto the fire escape with her diary and pen. Everything looked washed and sparkling, but not new, Birdie thought. She'd read too many bad novels to fall for that one, not anymore. She opened her diary and began to write:

The harbor looks very still. The air is clear and everything looks translucent and fragile. A scrap of low-lying mist wraps itself like a thin shawl around Castle Island. The sun's just slipping up somewhere behind me and my still, black water of a harbor—yes, okay, I'll concede to Homer on this morning of July 30 that it is even looking a little bit wine dark as the old rosy-fingered dawn spreads out there—this morning over there looks just about the same as over here. Washed, splendid, but not new. Not after what it has witnessed. Dewdrops, sun glints, shafts of light like arrows, veils of mist, etc., etc. It could all come out of a Carol Beth sample kit. It will never look fresh and new to me again, the way it's supposed to in books.

Is this some great tragedy that I, Bridget Rose Flynn, despite my scant sixteen years, now cannot look at a clear, pink dawn and see newness? See resurrection? Dad came out of the war with two favorite colors, an appreciation for ''Wop'' gardening skills and a lot of rollicking memories of the Joe Boy Team. Last night I read about evil, learned about evil. Real evil. It's nothing like TV evil, book evil, fairy-tale evil. It's not just that this evil is bloody. It's gray, too, and dingy and boring and ordinary—assembly-line evil of the death factories— Auschwitz, Treblinka, Dachau, Buchenwald. And it is not that they didn't know what they did and that they did not question it. It's something worse than that, that I can't explain. But when I read what Hoess said about ''having to watch children die,'' it is not as if he or any of them are going against their consciences. It is more as if they must overcome any feelings that are the least bit human. But even an animal would have more emotion, more feeling. Hoess is always talking about wearing this ''stony mask'' to hide his innermost feelings. Himmler said this incredible thing to his generals once— a little pep talk to get them through the carnage. I can't remember exactly, but he talked about what it was like to see hundreds and thousands of corpses, to ''have stuck it out . . . and at the same time to have remained de-

cent fellows," and then he talks about "this page of glory in our history"! None of these people ever once says, "I did it." It is always, "Look what I had to endure"! But how could all this evil happen side by side with good? How can there be such good and evil if there is a God? Did the SS—the Oberscharführer—send home Christmas and birthday cards to their families after having herded the daily thousands into the ovens? Did they think about their wives cooking stews over a gas flame while the smoke from their own stews belched from brick chimneys and fire scorched the sky? And here? Well, my mom was playing on Revere Beach and my dad was staking tomato plants as tall as small children, while other children and their mothers and fathers became ashes that were carried to rivers and washed away forever. It's all so weird. Isn't that a ridiculous word to use? That's the problem. No right words. Everything's changed, and now things (this is really awful to say, but I have to)—common things like soap and gold fillings for teeth—are like glass slivers from the slaughter. They seem to cut into me, push deeper. No more glass slippers, just slivers.

For several seconds she thought about crossing out the last sentence. But she let it stay.

Birdie stopped writing. The sun was up now. How had it dared, morning after morning? How could things have gone on—babies being born, trees blossoming? How could there be two such times within one time? The night before, Birdie had shouted in anger that she did not believe in God. Now without anger, and to no one, she whispered the words again.

CHAPTER

It was a kind of neutral place to be—Filene's basement. The conversation of hundreds of people, customers and salespeople, the respirations of the air conditioning system and the rumble of the subway a short distance away blended into a single, white thrum of noise. Birdie didn't really have to think or listen to anything she didn't want to. When the first tiny scratchings began, however, she was in the middle of selling a woman a pair of culottes with an overpanel, a compromise measure between a divided skirt and a regular one. At first she didn't really listen to the words. They were like little chicken claws scratching lightly, easily pushed aside. Birdie was actually thinking how much better the culottes would have looked on this woman if she could have worn them backward, so the overpanel would cover the woman's backside, which was large, to say the least. But then, of course, her stomach would show. Instead of an overpanel, what the woman needed was an "around panel." The scratchings came again, the little chicken feet, more definite this time. "I had to watch." What was it about those words? Who said them? Who else? She'd heard them before. Her forehead began to sweat.

"You all right?" the lady in the overpanel asked.

"Yeah, just a little headache." She wiped her forehead with the back of her hand. Why was she confused about those words? Two people had said them—Hoess's words, the ones she could not quite remember last night when she had been writing in her diary. Now they burst on her brain with a staggering force. Her hands moved mechanically as she took the woman's charge card, put it in the press and wrote the slip. She performed these small actions flawlessly, while out of the white noise that had filled her head and coated her brain the commandant's voice emerged clearly: "I had to look through the peephole and watch the process of death itself, because the doctors wanted me to see it . . . I had to watch closely." And Eichmann and Himmler—they, too, "had to . . ." and finally there was one other voice to be added. One other voice that had said it: ". . . had to . . . had to watch . . . had to watch them." Watch Mooch and Skeeter while they painted the swastikas, while he just made squiggles and slashes and some marks, "meaningless" marks, but he had had to watch. He was always just watching.

Her supervisor was very understanding. She ran up the basement stairs and left through the Washington Street exit. She cut through Winter Street to Tremont, crossed Tremont to the Common. The first park bench had a drunk asleep on it. Maybe he's trying to sleep off the last forty years, she thought. She didn't feel like sitting, anyway. She headed straight down through the Common till it met Charles Street. She crossed it and entered the Public Gardens. The swan boats paddled serenely with their cargo of well-mannered children. She tried to stop herself from thinking more, but her thoughts rushed ahead, chugged ahead like trainloads of children, swan boats of children, ovens of . . . . . Was Mrs. Pearlo-what with the numbers on her arm—was she a mother? Was her child sent to the left?

Birdie sat down hard on the bench. She stared at the swan boats. Did it matter whether they were wooden facsimiles or maybe real giant swans? In the last twenty-four hours things, words, events, had begun to break up for Birdie. Meaning was disintegrating. She could look at swan boats and see death trains. And gold fillings, blue gas flames and "solutions"— how could any of these things recover any sort of sane meaning? But was she to sit here on a park bench and try to retrieve such sanity as there was, had been? Some things defied understanding. The death camps were among them and so were the creatures who ran them. But there was one thing that Birdie had begun to understand, and that was the absolute corruption of the mind that says it has to watch, has to play a passive role in any kind of destruction. To watch and be silent was as evil as to pour the Zyklon crystals into the chambers where the innocents were gassed. That was the meaning of the words "I had to watch."

Birdie jumped up from the bench. She headed up Tremont

Street. On her left was the Kings Chapel graveyard, quiet and green and cool in the summer heat, the thin, gray stone markers testimonies to deaths gracefully done. Over the hill and down the other side of Tremont, Birdie walked at a pace just under a run. There was no way, she thought, that she could truthfully mourn six million people, grieve and cry for them all, but there was one person that she might be able to drag back, kicking and screaming, from the living dead. Tremont Street ended at Cambridge. She crossed it and started out across the vast brick expanse of the new City Hall. The faces of people streamed by her as offices let out for lunch. Were any of these people old enough to have been there? Did any of these people, so full of purpose now as they streamed toward their lunch dates, lose a grandparent, or an aunt, a cousin, a child? Did they know? Did they blame? Did they care?

Birdie turned into the marketplace. The stores with their elegant windows sparkled fiercely in the noon light. She saw it all and she saw nothing. She turned into Old Ironsides and whisked by the maître d'. "I'm here to see Timmy. Family emergency," she said, before he could ask her why she was there, and from the look on her face he decided it was better not to stop her from going back to the kitchen. She knew there wouldn't be any trouble from him. Restaurants like these didn't cope well with emergencies. The biggest emergency was when a waiter spilled something on a customer. If it was quiche, they came with a whisk broom and a damp cloth; anything messier, they came with a bottle of Perrier and napkins.

"What the hell is going on?" Timmy muttered as she propelled him out the back door of the kitchen into an alley. "What kind of emergency?"

"We'll talk down by the water."

"Is somebody dead?"

"Not yet."

"What are you talking about, Birdie? Are you trying to get me fired?"

She didn't answer, but kept walking. When they got to the end of India Wharf, Birdie turned and faced him.

"Is this about Phyllis, Birdie?"

"No!" she snapped. "I don't want to talk about Phyllis or Skeeter or Mooch. I want to talk about you and a monster named Rudolph Hoess, and a few others like him."

"Hoess?"

"Yeah. Ever heard of him?"

"No."

"Well, he was personally responsible for sending two million people to their deaths at a place called Auschwitz."

"Look, Birdie, if you're saying I'm like him just because I watched . . . ."

"Oh, no, Timmy, you're not going to get off that easy. I know the difference between killing and desecrating . . . ."

"So what are you saying I'm like Hoess for? I'm no killer."

"Yes, and Hoess himself never actually beat anyone or even with his own hands put the Zyklon crystals into the gas chambers. He just planned it all. 'Improved' it. That was the word he used in a confession. You see, he had gas chambers built that could hold two thousand people at a time, instead of two hundred. That's what he called an 'improvement,' Timmy."

97

"It's sick."

"Of course it is. You know what else he said, Timmy?" He shook his head but he didn't drop his eyes.

"Well, listen to this, 'cause here's another person who never actually did anything but just had to watch." The words came back to Birdie completely, in a torrent, but she spoke them carefully in measured time. " 'I had to watch coldly,' he said, 'while mothers with laughing or crying children went into the gas chambers—' "

"Birdie, I don't have to listen to this." Timmy turned away and Birdie reached out to clutch his arm.

"Just listen, Timmy! 'I had to see everything . . . the whole grisly, interminable business.' "

Timmy shook himself free. "Birdie! For God's sake, why are you doing this?"

But her voice rolled on strangely in a kind of hypnotic horror about mass graves and hair-cutting and chimneys. She paused a moment and this time Timmy did not interrupt. She reached out quietly and took his hand. He pressed it hard into a fist while she held it lightly. "And then, Timmy, he says, 'I had to look through the peephole.' Peephole," she repeated. Her voice grew small as if in wonder over the very sound of the word. " 'I had to look through the peephole of the gas chamber and watch the process of death itself.' "

For one horrible moment it was as if they felt themselves, both sister and brother, looking through the peephole of death. "Hoess said," Birdie continued, "that in order to do this he had to 'exercise intense self-control . . . in order to prevent my innermost doubts . . . I was forced to bury all human considerations as deeply as possible.' " Birdie stopped. She was still holding his hand.

"Timmy, I know you didn't kill, but how deeply did you have to bury your innermost doubts and feelings while you watched this 'prank'?"

Timmy looked directly at her, the communion between them unbroken. His skin was blotchy and red, but his eyes were like dark voids. "Birdie," he whispered, "it was real. I am the prank, and there is no place to bury anything in a prank."

CHAPTER 12

I didn't know what Timmy meant [Birdie wrote in her diary], *when he said that thing about him being the prank. It was as if he were saying he wasn't real. And . . . .*

She stopped writing for a full minute. Then she began again.

And I know this sounds weird, but it was almost as if he weren't real. His eyes were so shiny and blank. I remember reading once about those black holes in space that astronomers study, holes where everything like stars and matter and whole universes vanish and where none of the known laws of physics apply. That's what Timmy's eyes were like to me.

Birdie closed her diary. She got up and went to her closet, put on a clean shirt and began fluffing up her hair. The permanent still looked good. There was a knock on her door.

"Who is it?"

"Me." Lainie walked in, carrying her Carol Beth sample kit. "Where you going?"

"Gloria's."

"You're not grounded anymore?"

"No."

"You mean one night and that's it?" She blinked her pale blue eyes. The lids had been dabbed with something called Dusky Mauve, and Birdie thought it made them look like squashed grapes.

"Guess so," Birdie replied.

"Jeez, I got grounded for two months when Mom and Dad found out I was pregnant. In fact, I was grounded until the week before Richie and I were married." Lainie opened her eyes wide. "Come to think of it, I went straight from being grounded to being married."

"Wedded bliss," Birdie said and put on some lipstick.

"Hardly. But I just don't understand. One night for not believing in God. Two months for pregnancy. Do you believe again?"

"No."

"See? And with me they knew it wouldn't last forever. I mean, pregnancy can only go for nine months."

"So they say." Birdie was picking out her hair with a knitting needle she had borrowed from her mother. "Except

101

I read this thing in the *Guinness Book of World Records* about a lady who was pregnant for eleven and a half months. The baby weighed sixteen pounds at birth. Phew! Talk about being grounded.''

"Listen, do you have time to help me add up my sales and commissions before you go to Gloria's?"

"Do you have it all organized this time, Lainie? I can't fool around if all those slips are out of order."

"Don't worry. I've got it all in neat little piles, clipped together. See?" She took out a folder and all the yellow and pink slips were in separate stacks. "The ten-dollar-and-under orders on top, then the twenty-five-dollar ones and then the fifty-dollar ones and guess what?"

"What?" Birdie asked.

"Mrs. Di Grazie ordered one hundred and five dollars' worth of stuff."

"She needs it. Okay, let's get to it. The calculator's over there."

Lainie got the calculator and they both sat on the bed. "You read out the figures, Lainie, and I'll punch in. You have your p.o's all filled in except for the last column?"

"Yes."

Within ten minutes they had the figures recorded.

"Now for the fun part," Lainie said.

"Okay." Birdie handed her the calculator. "Now remember, when you figure the commissions . . ."

". . . the decimal point comes first," Lainie chimed in.
"Right."

In another five minutes Lainie had figured the commissions. "Now to add them up," she said excitedly. "It's going to be more than last week, I know."

"People gobble up that Exuberanza stuff, don't they?" Birdie said, looking over the order forms.

"It works. It really does. Most moisturizers just make you feel greasy, but this really works. You know Mrs. Fratiana?"

"Yeah."

"You should see how much better her wrinkles look with this stuff."

"But they're not gone?"

"Gone? Carol Beth is a cosmetician, not Jesus Christ!" Lainie immediately dropped her voice. Her eyes slid toward the door. "She looks better and at her age with her skin we don't ask for miracles, just improvements."

Birdie was looking intently at her sister. It was amazing what a little financial success could do for one's ego. What was wrong with herself? Why wasn't Filene's giving her such a boost? She looked back at the order forms. "You know what, Lainie! A lot of these people who ordered the moisturizer aren't anywhere near Mrs. Fratiana's age. They're young. How do you sell them this stuff?"

"Jet fumes," Lainie said matter-of-factly.

"Jet fumes? What are you talking about?"

"I tell them that the jet fumes from the airport make our skin age three times faster in East Boston."

"But is that true, Lainie?"

"I don't know."

"But, Lainie, it could be a lie."

"It's usually a sale, especially when I use words like

103

'emissions,' 'acidity' and 'embedded petroleum particles.'"

If Lainie had sprouted green hair on the spot she couldn't have surprised Birdie more than with this gush of polysyllabic words from her usually monosyllabic mouth.

" 'Embedded petroleum particles'—what the hell are those?"

"I don't know, but I bet the jets spray them on us all the time and they get under your skin and cause early dryness and collapse of delicate facial tissues."

Birdie touched her cheek lightly with her fingertips. "No kidding?"

"Yeah," Lainie continued. "You hear people talk about lovely English complexions. You don't hear them talking about lovely East Boston ones, do you?"

"No. That's right, I suppose."

"It's because they're gray. All communities that are this close to an airport have the problem. They probably don't have airports in England."

"I can't believe I'm having this conversation," Birdie said suddenly.

"But you are, and in another two minutes you might be buying a bottle of Exuberanza moisturizer. But you won't have to, because I'll give you this free sample for being such a good girl and helping me with the slips. You can also have some of that Desert Light blush. That's real popular here."

"Do they have something called Harbor Lights for the women in Phoenix?"

"Don't know, but you can have some of that Desert Light, or any other if you want. I have a lot of extra samples."

"Don't you want them?" Birdie asked.

"Woo—eee!" Lainie suddenly squealed. "Three hundred and seventy-five smackers. No, I don't need any Desert Light for a divorce. All I need is money."

"You must have enough by now."

"Well, you've got your lawyer's fee and your filing charges and then court costs."

Birdie once more was absolutely astounded by her sister. Lainie's doughy face with the almost translucent eyes shadowed with mauve powder looked keen and alert. Birdie stared at her hard. She thought she had known this person all her life, inside out, but suddenly she felt as if she were being confronted by a stranger, some odd creature, a cross between Carol Beth and Clarence Darrow.

"How do you know all this law stuff, Lainie?"

"I found out mostly from Angela. She's had two."

"Two what?"

"Divorces. What are you looking at me that way for?"

"Oh, nothing, nothing."

"Yes, you were," Lainie persisted.

"Oh, just your eyeshadow, I guess. How come you chose that color? All those others are so much nicer. Tawny Sunset, Dawn on Pearls."

"I know." Lainie laughed and blushed.

"So why don't you try them?"

Lainie's shoulders dropped and she smiled crookedly. "I guess you can say that I'm sort of attached to this color."

"What are you talking about? Attached to a color?"

"Well, it's identical to the color my skin gets when Richie punches me."

"You're kidding," Birdie said softly. She didn't know whether to laugh or cry.

"No," Lainie replied brightly. "And I can't have him noticing too much. I mean, he still doesn't know I'm doing all this." She gestured at the pink vinyl kit. "You don't see me going around with that Red-As-All-Get-Out lipstick on or the nail polish or the mascara."

"Yeah," Birdie said.

"It makes sense, doesn't it? I mean, I've got to wear something when I sell. It won't look as if I believe in the product if I don't, will it?"

"Yeah, I guess so."

"I just sort of arrange the bruises a little. Same color. Just neater. He never notices." She giggled.

"Well, what'll you do if he gives you another one? They aren't so neat to begin with."

"Aha!" Lainie exclaimed. "The Carol Beth neutral cover-up. Goes on any skin tone. Unless you're colored, of course, and we'll have a cover-up for them soon. Anyhow, that's why I've got to get more money than for just the divorce. Because before I even go to court I gotta get me and Rhonda into an apartment where he won't find us, because you can imagine what he'll do to me when I file!"

"File?"

"That's what you call it when you start the proceedings."

"Oh," Birdie said.

They finished up the accounting. Lainie put the sample kit into Birdie's lower bureau drawer and they went downstairs together. They stopped briefly on the walkway by the chipped madonna.

106

"Where you going now?" Lainie asked. "Gloria's?"

"Yeah. Where're you going?"

"McDonald's with Rhonda."

"Where're you going?" Birdie said, suddenly cocking her head toward the madonna.

"Who are you talking to?"

"Our Lady of Perpetual Weeds over there."

"You nuts?"

Birdie smiled. Lainie started to laugh. "She ain't going nowhere, Birdie. Not with those weeds. She's stuck right here!"

"I know," Birdie said quietly. "Well, see you."

CHAPTER

The crisp white café curtains billowed like tiny sails as a fresh sea breeze blew through the windows in the Saccarellis' kitchen.

"I've read five hundred romances in the past two years, from Barbara Cartland to Janet Dailey. I know I can do it." Rose Saccarelli spoke firmly. "I know thousands of other women say they can write these things, too. Well, I'm one of them, and I'm not going to sit around any longer. Gloria got me a new ribbon for the typewriter and I started last night. Vinnie says that if I stick to it and finish one book, even if I don't sell it, he'll buy me an airline ticket to the romance-writers' convention in Houston."

"And"—Vinnie called in from the living room—"if she finishes three chapters, I'll buy her a bottle of—what's it called, Rosie?"

"Ciarissima."

"That's it—Ciarissima perfume—and if she finishes eight chapters, a negligee set." Vinnie had walked into the kitchen and was leaning against the doorjamb. "And for the book, it's Houston, here we come! It's called S.W.I.P. The Saccharelli Writing-Incentive Program."

"Sounds great," Birdie said. "So what's the book about?"

"Well, it takes place in Boston. I figure I'll set this one here so I won't have to do a lot of research, this being my first one and all."

"By the time she writes number five," Vinnie interjected, "we'll be able to finance research to places like Honolulu, right?"

"Don't kid, Vinnie. Anyway, it takes place in Boston and it's about a girl in her late teens who becomes pregnant by a Beacon Hill type."

"Just don't name them Cabot or Lodge. I don't want any lawsuits."

"No, I'm going to name them something like Randall. Anyway, the girl gets pregnant and has the baby, but she never tells him. It's basically, I think, a Forget-Me-Not–type book."

"A what?" Birdie asked.

"A Forget-Me-Not. That's a line. Every publisher calls their romance-category books something special. Like Candlelight Ecstasy, Rapture, Forget-Me-Not, Second Chance at Love. Each line has different guidelines and requirements."

"Tell her about the sex guidelines, Ma," Gloria interrupted.

"Oh, Gloria, you're fixated," her mother replied.

"I'm fixated! You're the one writing the book."

"Yeah. What are the sex guidelines? I'm fixated, too," Vinnie said.

"Well," Rose began, "some have no touching below the neck, some below the waist . . . ."

"Some in between the ears," Vinnie offered.

"Vinnie!"

"Vinnie!" Gloria and Birdie both echoed.

"Well," Rose continued, "I didn't want those kinds of limitations."

"Ooh! Raunchy Mom!"

"It's not raunchy, Gloria. I just need some room to move around."

"Woo—eee!" Vinnie hooted and rolled his eyes.

"It will be 'tastefully handled.' Those are the exact words from the guidelines. Here, I'll read them to you." She reached for a book on the kitchen counter entitled: *The Road to Romance: How to Write a Category Book*. "It says right here in the 'Guidelines for Forget-Me-Not Books,' published by M. Charpentier Publications, that 'lovemaking and nudity are acceptable as long as tastefully handled. Focus should be on erotic sensations, arousal by kisses and caresses, rather than mechanics of sexual acts. Steamy and erotic tone is suitable. Anything kinky is out.' "

"In other words," said Birdie, "smouldering but not mouldering."

"You see!" Rose gestured toward Birdie. "You should be

110

writing these, not me. You have such a way with words, Birdie.''

"Well, on with the story. What happens next?"

"She comes from a poor family, not Beacon Hill."

"Please don't make it East Boston," Birdie said.

"No. Don't worry. Gloria already made me promise that. I think it'll be Dorchester.''

"Okay," said Birdie. "Then what?"

"Well, she has the baby and he never knows and she just fades out of his life, and, oh, I forgot to tell you—he was going with another girl at the time."

"Creep!" Birdie said.

"Well, she was a debutante and his parents were, you know, all for her and he was engaged to her."

"What a turkey!" Birdie wrinkled her nose.

"Well, he had to, you know. His parents and all."

"People *have* to get married, not engaged," Birdie said.

"Well, you see, his parents have all this money and his family owns . . . ." At this point Vinnie rolled his eyes toward the ceiling. "If this gets me fired, Rosie!"

"He always gets nervous at this part."

"Why?" Birdie was enjoying this talk immensely.

"Just wait till you hear this!" Vinnie muttered.

"Now, calm yourself, Vinnie. The names will be entirely different. You see"—Rose said, turning again to Birdie—"the family owns a newspaper, but . . ." She turned back to her husband and spoke very slowly, in cadences one might use to assure a young child that everything will be all right. "We're not going to call it the *Globe*."

"And not the *Universe* or the *World*, Rosie! That's too close.

All the names in creation and Rosie chooses the *World*."

"No, I have a new name," she said.

"What?" Vinnie asked.

"The *Standard*. Not even the *Boston Standard*. So nobody will ever complain."

Vinnie squinted one eye slightly in contemplation. "Well, maybe, but couldn't you just change the family business?"

"No, I can't. It has to be this. It's more romantic."

"There is nothing, I tell you, romantic about the newspaper business, absolutely nothing. I may be just a pressman, but I know what goes on in the city room. It's no more romantic there than where I am. It's pressure, deadlines, morning and evening editions, it's union hassles."

"Well, what do you want for a family business, Dad—a plumbing empire?"

"I'd feel easier, believe me!"

"Oooh! Maybe I'll do plumbing for my next one." Rose's eyes sparkled. "I thought I'd like to do a Regency story."

"What's that?" Birdie asked.

"Kings, queens, courts—you know. I'll call it *Royal Flush*!" Everyone groaned except Rose, who was quite taken by her little pun.

"I want to hear the rest of the plot. So you've got this pregnant girl and this newspaper family and the pregnant girl—what's her name, so I don't have to keep calling her the pregnant girl?"

"Margaret, I think."

"So Margaret has disappeared, had her baby?"

"Disappeared for quite a while and Randall marries the

debutante, Lacey. Isn't that a great name for a debutante? I'm very proud of that. Gloria, can you get me a Lite beer?"

"Get me a fat one," Vinnie called out as Gloria headed for the refrigerator.

"That is good, Mrs. Saccharelli. They always have names like that—Poo and Moo, Bitsey, Lacey, Bambi."

Vinnie took a swallow of beer and stifled a burp. "Who's their father—Walt Disney?"

"Vinnie!"

"Okay. On with the story," Birdie urged. "He's married Lacey."

"And Margaret has had her child, gotten some more education, and gone to work for another small newspaper. So, to make a long story short, through a combination of hard work and intelligence, she rises to the top. The newspaper grows, giving the *Standard* a run for its money. By this time she's editor, but of course, Randall, who is publisher of the *Standard*, never dreams that this can be the same Margaret Perry from Dorchester and he is going to try to hire her or maybe buy the whole newspaper. Meanwhile, Lacey has turned out to be a real disaster, nasty and a nincompoop. So—" Rose paused.

"So?" Birdie asked.

"Well, that's as far as I've gotten. I'll figure out the rest."

Birdie was sure that she would. As she walked down the street from the Saccharellis', Birdie suddenly felt sad. Everybody seemed to be headed somewhere. Lainie, with her pocketful of money for divorce court, Mrs. Saccharelli for Houston with intermediate stops at the perfume counter and lingerie, everybody except her and Timmy! She hadn't even seen him since she'd left him crying on India wharf. She turned abruptly and headed back toward the corner, crossed the street and started walking toward Our Lady of Victory. It was just one minute after quitting time.

"But, Father! No fair! No fair!" And there was the stamp of a foot, but it was much heavier than a child's.

"Now, now, Benny." A deep, resonant voice that certainly wasn't Timmy's spoke. Birdie was in the basement halfway down the corridor from the maintenance supply room.

"But I just can't help it. I mean, all these years I've been the only one to—" Birdie couldn't hear the rest of the phrase.

"Poor Benny!" the voice said.

"Well, my feelings are hurt."

"Now, everything is going to be all right."

"Look"—it was Timmy's voice—"I won't do it again. I was only trying to help out."

What has he done now? Birdie thought. It couldn't have been so bad, because the other voice—Father Leo's—was saying something about its being no one's fault as Benny blubbered on in a sickening sort of baby talk. Birdie decided to make her presence known immediately and give everyone time to pull themselves together before they saw her. "Timmy!" she called out. "You still here?"

A few seconds later Timmy, Benny and Father Leo came into the corridor.

"Your bwuder did something a teeny bit naughty!"

114

"Oh, what was that?" asked Birdie, her voice drenched in indifference.

"Now, Benny, we've been all through this," Father Leo sighed. "It was not naughty. Timmy merely replaced the votive candles when some worshipper found the box empty and asked for more when Benny was outside."

"But he should have asked me first and not gotten the keys from my desk without permission."

"Sorry. I won't ever do it again."

Father Leo shot Birdie and Timmy an understanding glance over Benny's head.

"See you tomorrow, Tim. You're Tim's sister, Bridget Rose, aren't you?" he said, turning to her. "I haven't seen you for some time. Not since confirmation days."

"Yeah. I guess it has been a long time," Birdie replied.

"Well, it's nice to see you again."

They walked into the alley behind the church. "I mean, really, Timmy, that Benny is sick, really sick! That scene in there was absolutely nauseating, not even pathetic, just plain nauseating. How often does Benny use baby talk?"

"Only around Father Leo. Kind of trying to be a teacher's pet, I guess."

"Yuck! I don't know how you stand it. Teacher's pet! More like the worm in the apple for the teacher. Oh well, turn here. I nearly forgot I promised Mom I'd pick up something at the cleaners."

The shop was crowded with people picking up cleaning on

their way home from work. There were two lines of customers as Birdie and Timmy waited their turn. Neither one of them noticed the plump, gray-haired woman next to them. But just as Birdie was stepping up to the counter to give the girl the yellow slip, another girl behind the counter came up with a hanger of cleaning. Birdie didn't exactly know what happened first—the numbers or the name, but all of a sudden the other girl behind the counter was saying, "Here, Mrs. Pearlowitz." An arm went out to reach for the cleaning, and Birdie saw the small inky marks just above the wrist on the underside. Everything stopped for Birdie that moment. She could read the marks clearly—498832—the nameless numbers of the death camp. It was incomprehensible to see a human being numbered this way. Birdie stared. In their tiny fastidiousness, the marks appeared like stitchery or a kind of sickening embroidery. She stared and stared. Whistles screeched. It could have been Maverick Square, East Boston or it could have been a camp, but it was no longer a page printed in a book she had read.

"*Zahlappell!* Roll call!" a hoarse voice shouted in her mind. "*Alles aufstehen zum Zahlappell.* All up for roll call." It was three in the morning. Shivering in the mud and drizzle, they formed into groups of five. A cloying smell of burning fat hung in the air as a horrible dawn glowed red in the west. But the rest of the sky was black, not a slip of moonlight, not a squeak from God.

Then it was over.

"Are you Mrs. Pearlowitz . . . from the synagogue?" Just

as they had walked out the door, Timmy had touched her lightly on the arm. She stopped and faced them and Birdie saw that she knew who they were. Timmy ran his fingers through his hair. "I . . . I . . . I don't know how to say this. I'm not even sure why I'm saying this, but I want to tell you something." He thrust his hands into his jeans pockets to stop them from moving around. Birdie didn't know what was happening, but within the space of two minutes things had changed in some small way forever. But Timmy kept talking—fast and scatty, his feet moving, his hands in and out of his pockets. "Everything I've done . . ." He paused. It was a painful and interminable pause. He began again, "Everything I've done up till now . . . it was, like, you know, wrong—all wrong. It's like that king guy in the fairy tale who touched things and they turned to gold. Well, everything I touch, do, make, well . . ." He stopped and pressed his fist to his chin. "Wait a minute, just a minute."

It was like watching a person gasping for oxygen or a fish for water. But Mrs. Pearlowitz waited. She waited like nothing Birdie had ever seen wait. She waited like a rock.

"This wasn't magic, Mrs. Pearlowitz. I'm not trying to get out of this. I did it. I did it! I hate that I did it, but I did it. I'm sorry." His hands unclenched. His feet were still. "There's no right words for me. No right words to apologize. I can't say that I had no idea of what you've been through or who you are, because even if that were true it doesn't make it right. And what you have been through, if I let myself think, is"— he paused—"I was going to say incredible, but I believe it." Timmy was looking directly at the tattooed numbers on Mrs. Pearlowitz's arm. "I mean, I believe this all happened but it is too incredible to be able to understand, is what I really mean."

"It is beyond understanding," Mrs. Pearlowitz whispered, but she was looking straight at Timmy. Her eyes had a sadness that neither Birdie or Timmy had ever really seen before in a person. It was a sadness that separated her and her kind of survivor from the rest of the world. "Now, you must know one thing." She spoke with a quiet fierceness. "I don't want your pity or your apology. There is no way you can weep for six million of us, but you can believe it happened. You do believe it happened. And you see something in my eyes that makes them different, like a dead person's, maybe, looking out. That will never change. And in the middle of the night my neighbors say they can sometimes hear me scream. They used to think I was afraid of something. But I tell you now I am beyond fear. I scream because of rage, not fear. Rage, not revenge. Rage for the dead. Rage for those who do not believe this happened and rage for myself."

There was another silence. Then Timmy spoke. "I believe you, Mrs. Pearlowitz."

"Good," she rasped.

"And"—Timmy took a deep breath—"I hate the part of me that did this."

"So do I." She turned and walked away.

CHAPTER 14

I would like to say [Birdie wrote a few days later in her diary], *I mean, isn't this the way it's supposed to be in books, that Mrs. Pearlowitz invited us in for cookies and milk and that we all became good friends? We would have one of those cozy relationships that springs up between old people and misunderstood youths. We would share our small, little triumphs and problems. I would run errands for her, and Timmy would repair stuff around her apartment and lift things for her that were too heavy for an old lady to lift. The problem is this: Mrs. Pearlowitz has an unshareable past that somehow makes her present unshareable except perhaps with a very few, and* as for heavy things to lift, she is forever bent and crooked from forty years of carrying the heaviest load of all. So there is nothing we can do for each other. I knew this. Timmy knew it and, of course, Mrs. Pearlowitz knew it. So what else can I say? Why did Timmy do it? Why did he go up to her like that in the first place? Who knows? I wanted to talk to him about it on the way home but he sealed right up. But something really has changed. I felt it in the shop with Timmy, and he told me on the way home that he's got a new job. Took my advice. He's working for the Petersens—deckhand on the tug. Maybe I should go into employment counseling. I've started Lainie on the road to riches. Well, if not started her, at least helped her manage the finances. Except now she's really learning how to do the math. And here's Timmy quitting the dishwashing and going on the tug. He's really excited. First time I've ever see him this way.

I went down to the pier yesterday, late afternoon. I thought I'd find him there. He wasn't there, at least not on our pier. He was two down where the tugs tie up. He was just sort of standing there leaning against a piling, real relaxed, talking with Captain Petersen about something. I could have called over to him, but I don't know, I just didn't. Didn't feel like it, I guess. But it was real funny. I could tell just by the way he was standing that he was looking right at Mr. Petersen and talking to him. I've never seen him do this before, except with me. When Timmy talks to people, he talks to their feet.

Elsewhere on the employment front I've become a drop-in editor for Mrs. Saccharelli as she churns out Deadline for Love. I read the first three chapters. They're

120

*okay. I mean, Ernest Hemingway she isn't, but I guess
in this romance-novel stuff she's as good as the next.
She's a little long winded in places, so I cut her. She
sure doesn't know grammar. That's my main job—dig-
ging out dangling participles and breaking them down
into logical sentences. She doesn't understand dangling
participles at all, and she keeps writing them. I guess
it's just a case of her seeing everything so clearly that
she never doubts that the rest of the world will, too. For
example, she wrote this thing about their eyes latching
across the Public Gardens. It went something like this:
"Walking across the Public Gardens, their eyes latched
in front of the Ritz." I could just see these four eyeballs
rolling lickety-split across the garden, through the pe-
tunia beds and the pansy rings, across the pathways,
dodging kids on skateboards and plop-plop-plop-plop into
the duck pond. Enough to make the swan boats sprout
wings and take off. No more cutie-pie children's stories
about little duck families. "Yuck!" say the ducks.
"Yuck!" "Yuck!" say Mr. and Mrs. Mallard. "Yuck!"
"Yuck!" "Yuck!" "Yuck!" "Yuck!" "Yuck!" "Yuck!"
"Yuck!" say Jack, Kack, Lack, Mack, Nack, Ouack,
Pack and Quack. "Here's looking at you, four-eyes!"
says Humphrey Bogart. Anyway, Mrs. Saccharelli needs
an editor to save her from these potentially embarrass-
ing moments.*

"Birdie!" It was Timmy outside her door.

"Yeah?"

Timmy poked his head in. "You still want to go get a
pizza?"

"Yes. I'm off my diet today."

"How come? You're always dieting."

"I know, so I decided to go off today." Boys, Birdie thought, could never understand how girls could eat when they weren't hungry, just down. And Birdie was down. No doubt about it. She felt lousy and she didn't know why.

"I've got to stop at the church first. I have an appointment with Father Leo to rearrange my hours."

"It's okay. I'll come anyway." Amazing the things one would agree to do to get a pizza when one finally went off a diet, Birdie thought.

Timmy had been inside with Father Leo about two minutes and Birdie had been waiting outside the office door thinking about a mushroom-and-pepperoni pizza when Benny Arlette came down the hall.

"What are you doing here, Birdie?"

"Waiting for Tim."

"Timmy in there?" He gestured with his head toward the door.

"Yeah."

The baby-doll mouth twisted and curled. The pink slits opened wider for the little pig eyes. "What's he doing in there with Father Leo?"

"I don't know." God, Birdie thought, he's ruining my pizza, although she knew there was no such thing as wrecking the anticipation of a pizza once a dieter's resolve had been broken. It was an anticipation that had little to do with real hunger. Benny had not ruined the pizza prospect. She was ashamed to admit that if even Benny Arlette had said, "Come down to the maintenance room—I've got hot fudge sundaes,'' she would probably join him, sit right down with this loathsome little pudge of a man and pig out. Right now, however, Benny was planted firmly in front of her and Birdie was not in the mood for light conversation. She had absolutely nothing to say to him. So she tapped her toe on the floor and thought about Phyllis Dougherty. She thought about soft ice cream after the pizza. She thought about funny dangling participles she had known. She glanced occasionally at the office door and gradually began to think about how she was standing outside in the hallway with the losers. She nearly gasped out loud as the realization crept over her. The door burst open and Father Leo and Timmy stepped out. They were smiling. Father Leo had his hand on Timmy's shoulder. Benny glowered like a hateful cherub.

"Hello, Birdie," Father Leo said. "Well, Tim and I have it all worked out. We're shifting his hours a bit, Benny. He's taken another job, and he'll just work twelve hours a week now, six on Sundays through late Mass."

"But—" Benny began to sputter.

"Don't worry, Benny," Timmy said. "I'm just going to do the vacuuming and the restrooms—that stuff."

"You'll do your usual," Father Leo added. "The vestments, the altar, the holy water, the candles."

"Well, I should hope so," huffed Benny, but there was resignation in his voice.

Birdie felt like asking if anybody really cared who put the holy water into the basin—Pig Winks, Father Leo or Timmy? But she had to admit that Timmy had handled the situation

123

beautifully with Benny. Diplomatically, one might even say. Benny's ruffled feathers had not only been smoothed but the whole situation had changed. He was still to have his holy water and candles, his altar detail and vestments to check, but he didn't have Timmy.

CHAPTER 15

They had finished the pizza and were heading up Orleans Street. Birdie took a lick of her ice cream. "I want to stop at the Store Twenty-four and pick up some coffee cake."

"Boy, when you go off your diet, you really go off!"

"Hmmm." She didn't want to talk about it. "Tell me something. What exactly has to be done with holy water?"

"Pour out the old water into a special sink, clean the basin, put in the new, I guess. I don't know, seeing as I never worked there on Sundays before and Benny always does it. Why'd you ask?"

"Just wondered. You told Mom and Dad about your latest job yet?"

Timmy studied his sister for a moment. "You pissed?" he asked.

"No. Why? I just asked if you told Mom and Dad."

"Not yet."

"Why not?"

"The Petersens aren't union."

"Uh-oh!"

"Yep. I don't know how Dad will take to that."

"I do, unfortunately. Do me a favor, Timmy."

"What's that?"

"Don't tell them tonight. Mom's making fried chicken and lemon meringue pie. I don't want a good dinner ruined."

Some five and a half pounds and two days later, Birdie was sipping a diet soda and very quietly watching her family. Rhonda, of course, was watching another family on television, the Smurfs, the strange, little blue gnomish figures that had captured the hearts of millions of kids under the age of ten and were making millions of dollars for their creators. They were smurfing along, but unbeknownst to them their deadly enemy Gargamel had prepared a most un-Smurfly brew. One little Smurfette (a girl Smurf) was about to drink it on a picnic.

"Watch it. She'll turn green," Rhonda said without taking her eyes from the screen.

"Better than blue, I think," Birdie said.

"No. They die if they're green."

"But I just don't understand, Timmy," Marge was saying. "You go out. You get this job. You don't discuss it with either

126

of us. I mean, after all, you're paying your father back from these jobs and—''

''I know that.'' Timmy shifted uneasily but remained calm. ''It's a better job. More money.''

''But the hours, Timmy!''

''That's not it, Marge. It's not the hours,'' Joe said.

''Well, what is it, Dad?'' Timmy's voice carried none of the familiar sullenness, and only the slightest tension. ''Is it the union thing?''

Birdie kept her eyes on the Smurfs, but she listened intently to her own family. Something was happening and she could not put her finger on it. It felt as if everybody's relationship to one another in the family was about to change or already starting to. Maybe they were all going to turn blue or green or whatever it was. Maybe they would each turn a different color from Dawn on Pearls to Dusky Mauve. She sipped her diet soda steadily and watched the little Smurfette.

''Yeah,'' said Joe belligerently. ''I'll give you that. I'm not overjoyed with the idea of you working nonunion. You ain't no dummy on that score.''

Timmy remained calm. Joe looked at his son, baffled, searching for another response. ''I'm—'' Joe began to speak, then paused and swallowed, seemingly at a loss for words. Maybe it was because before, he merely had to yell to begin a fight that Timmy always lost. Birdie almost felt sorry for her dad. ''I'm not,'' he began again, ''going to say no.''

As soon as Joe had spoken that phrase, sentence, that negative declaration, Birdie knew what was going on in the room. It was not that Joe was not going to say no; he couldn't say no. He couldn't say no, because he was beginning to perceive the first glimmerings of a new kind of strength and independence that he did not in the least understand. It was not the physical strength that stood one well on the streets or insured one's supremacy in the house. It was something else and it was scary to Marge and to Joe. Birdie could see it in their faces.

"But, Joe—" Marge started to speak but couldn't finish.

"But what?" he barked. "What do you want me to do, Marge?"

"Well, do you think this is right?"

"No! I don't think this is right at all," he shouted, and then abruptly walked out of the room into the bedroom and slammed the door.

"See what you've done to your father?"

"Mom, he didn't do it," Birdie said.

"You stay out of it, missy!" Marge was shaking her finger. Her face was white and grim. "What do you know about union? Well, I'll tell you. Your father wouldn't work for Mr. Goldman before they went union. Mr. Goldman had asked him and asked him, but no way."

"But, Ma," Timmy said, "it's not that important in the harbor. I mean, with Dad it's trucks and trucks mean teamsters' union. But this is tugboats. It's just not the same."

"The men in our family have always been union."

"But that's no reason," Birdie said, "to do something just because people have always done it."

"It was a good enough reason for your father and his father and my father."

"It's no reason!"

"Would you shut up, Birdie!" Marge barked. She turned toward Timmy and looked at him as if she were trying to figure out not so much what to say but how to say it. "Oh, Lord!" she muttered and threw down a tissue she had wadded in her hands.

"You going to church, Mom?" Birdie asked as her mother headed out the door.

"No, I need a pack of cigarettes."

Definitely weird [Birdie wrote in her diary]. *I don't know what to make of it. Everybody's doing things differently. No blowup. No rosaries. I guess it's really hard to go to church and pray about the union. It would make you feel a little bit funny. I mean, suppose somebody just lit a candle for a kid who's got leukemia and there you are, lighting one for a son who's nonunion? This sounds funny to say, but tonight it feels like there's this big hole right smack in the middle of our family. Mom came back with her cigarettes. Dad came out to watch the news and Timmy was here, too, but we all just sort of sat there. I mean, I can't say that we were the Waltons before and none of us is what you'd call a sparkling conversationalist, but somebody always at least had something to say about what was happening on television. We occasionally said a word to one another and somebody was always getting mad at Timmy. As a matter of fact, a lot of my conversation was screaming "shut up" to them while they were yelling at Timmy, so I could do my homework. Even the other night, Lainie, of all people, screeches out of the bedroom for people to shut up. She can't concentrate to figure out her commissions. Well, it wasn't that way tonight. You couldn't concentrate because of the silence. At one point I looked up. We were all sitting there. Lainie had just come in. Mom, Dad, Timmy and myself, Rhonda half-asleep on the couch— we were all watching this special that was on television and I thought to myself, Why are these six people sitting here in this room together? All of a sudden it wasn't like family. It was just like six random people in a room watching television.*

CHAPTER 16

"Want to cruise designer sportswear? All the fall clothes are in now." Gloria had just come over on break.

"Sure. Anything to escape the fragrance of this hot dog stand. Somehow, hot dogs and better bags don't mix."

"You're right. I don't know why they put all this next to a hot dog stand," Gloria said, poring over a pile of handsome leather bags.

"Cows and pigs, I guess."

"Oh, Birdie! How gross."

"Pardon me," she said, putting on her linen blazer. "Cows and pork byproducts."

"That sounds worse. Come on, let's go."

131

Fall clothes never seemed to change that much, Birdie thought. Plaids and corduroys, wool-blend pants and gabardines, crew necks, cowl necks and turtleneck sweaters to wear under smart, tweedy jackets. And then, of course, the irresistible high leather boots. There was something about fall clothes, just looking at them, that had always excited Birdie, that conjured up images of crisp autumn days to come and kindled resolutions of hard work and high purpose. But today it didn't happen. The prospect of school starting did not thrill her. Her grades were okay, and even if she did get better grades, where was she going to go with them? Harvard? What would she do there, anyway? She didn't know any longer what, if anything, she wanted to have or do. Even now, as she and Gloria wandered from department to department on the fourth floor, she was not sure where she was walking or what she was looking for. Gloria, on the other hand, was putting together outfits, making a list so when the clothes hit the basement she would be there ready to pounce. So here was Gloria full of energy and purpose, negotiating her way through the racks and stacks of fall clothes. Timmy, too, was full of energy these days, at least whenever she saw him. Those times had been rare, however, in the last two weeks since he had been working for the Petersens aboard the *Neptune*. Every evening and two mornings a week, he would come home exhausted and either hole up in his room or go to his job at Our Lady of Victory after a quick nap. Only because Birdie had caught him yesterday morning as he came in from work was she going to see him today. He had promised her that if she got to the Charlestown pier by 5:30 she could watch them bring in a

132

tanker and then get on board for the hop across to East Boston.

"Okay. What do you think?" Gloria twirled around in the black velveteen blazer and held up a brown plaid skirt to her waist. "Birdie!"

"Oh, sorry. I wasn't paying attention. Uh, that's nice, but don't you think the black is a little formal?"

"Not with the brown. The brown softens it. I think it's very elegant—black and brown. Those are the new colors for fall."

"Oh," said Birdie.

"What's with you? It's like you're off in some other world. You should be looking at this stuff, too. We're going to be out of the basement and on two by October and you've got to look the part." Look the part, Birdie thought. What part? She was always looking, she thought suddenly, and not being. And as for moving up to the second floor, so far the moves had been more horizontal than vertical—Birdie from separates to bags, and Gloria from underwear to outerwear, but they were still in the basement.

Between break and the time she got off for lunch, Birdie had sold almost two thousand dollars' worth of handbags. She hadn't even had to try very hard. She was learning that people mostly sold themselves on a thing, and the people who came to better bags in the basement were either trying to look a part or already were a part. They were aiming for a kind of tailored chic that seemed to be embodied in the feel and smell of good leather. Too bad the hot dog stand interfered with the smell of good leather, but it didn't seem to inhibit anyone's buying. Gloria even bought one with her store discount in anticipation of her black velveteen blazer and brown skirt.

At 5:25, Birdie was standing on a pier in Charlestown. A huge tanker in the channel began to swing slowly toward the pier, and when it had swung forty degrees or so, a tiny tug was revealed nestled against its starboard side. Birdie watched with growing fascination as the tug nudged and guided and tugged and poked the huge ship. She had seen tankers and tugs all her life, but this interplay between the giants and the dwarfs she had never really looked at. It was like a slow-moving dance between a most unequal pair. But they danced well together. What the tanker lacked in agility was provided by the tug, which, with its blunt-nosed power, could guide and push through channels and into berths. Birdie became slowly aware of two figures on the deck of the *Neptune* handling lines. One was stationary, but the other moved swiftly from bow to stern. The glare of the sun on the metallic water made the figures appear as silhouettes, only distinguishable to Birdie now by the fact that one moved and the other remained still. As the ship came closer, the moving figure actually seemed to sprint the deck length of the tug. Suddenly the figure leaped, leaped so high that it was clear of the gunwales and printed for one fraction of a second against the sky in a glorious extension—with muscle and sinew taut and poised as a dancer's. The air seemed to hold the figure for that split second in time. The shirt was orange. It was Timmy.

"Sit up on the forward bollard." Eve Petersen nodded toward an upright post with a horizontal outcropping. "You'll get a nice view and the last of the day's sun. We don't serve drinks. This is no cocktail cruise but there's some leftover cake

134

from dinner, if you want it. That is, if the bottomless pit over there hasn't consumed it." She raised her brows and looked in Timmy's direction. Birdie sat straddling the horizontal part of the bollard, her head resting against the vertical part. The tug had swung around back into the channel and now was heading toward its berth in East Boston. Because the trip was so short, Eve and Timmy were busy arranging lines for tying up. Everybody worked with purpose and economy of motion. Even the tug itself, steered by Morrie Petersen, seemed to take the shortest swing of an arc when turning to maneuver. No wonder, Birdie thought, that children loved tugboats. What could be more interesting to them than little things pushing big things around? Once more Birdie was struck by the quickness and grace of her brother's movement. He was even better than Eve Petersen, who had been doing this for years. They valued him—Birdie could tell. She could tell this by the way both Petersens looked at him after they tied up and were all below having a beer and talking about the day's jobs. She could tell by the way they joked with him and talked about tomorrow's jobs—the freighter from Halifax and the Oslo tanker due in. She watched as Morrie Petersen meticulously described each ship to Timmy—its tonnage, length, hull, any peculiarities.

"The Halifax ship has a more turbulent bow wave than the tanker. Let me look at the papers here . . ." He reached behind him for a clipboard. "She's coming in nearly empty. So you're going to get a lot of shimmying if it's windy."

"Where do they usually carry half-cargo on a ship like that?"

"Let's hope it's stowed low."

"You can't count on it, Morrie. Last time he came in here he didn't and it took us by surprise. I think we should use those number-three lines. Don't you, Timmy?

"Yeah, and maybe have an extra in reserve."

"Good idea." Eve Petersen nodded. "You're right."

CHAPTER
17

"*You're right!*" [Birdie wrote] *Nobody has ever, I bet, told Timmy he's right or, for that matter, that he has had a good idea. Timmy is supposed to be wrong and have no ideas. Now not only is he right and has bright ideas, but hang onto your hat, diary, if you wear one— I guess I should say hang onto your metaphorical hat— Timmy is studying navigation! Timmy, who reads on a fourth-grade level, who can hardly manage long division. Timmy of the three F's and a D is, I repeat, studying navigation and has been for the last three and a half weeks. He's halfway through the second chapter and to quote him, "It's getting easier since my reading's picked up." He's been doing it secretly, mostly in his bedroom. He hid the book from Ma in the back of his closet.*

Elsewhere in the personal growth department, how can we forget that other closet case, namely my sister, the one who got pregnant in high school and had to scrap plans for the convent? Well, she has just been given a little pin from the Carol Beth people for the highest sales of the month. By Christmas she should be an area manager and within a hair's breadth of a divorce. Let's see . . . and Gloria feels that by Christmas time, although our moves thus far have been strictly lateral at Filene's, we should be on the second floor. Ascension is suspension (of belief) for me. Our progress report would be incomplete without an update from the literary quarter. Mrs. Saccharelli will, in another half-chapter, find herself on the third floor, in lingerie, more specifically negligees. She's already collected the bottle of Ciarissima. In short, everybody seems to know exactly where they are going and getting there except me! Do I sound jealous? I am. But the saddest is this: I don't know what to be jealous for or of. Do I really want to write what Mrs. Saccharelli is writing—"Their eyes latched . . . he thrust against her." "Thrust," by the way, is the in verb on the romance-novel circuit—less technical than "penetrate," more virile than "push." A word that one might say has that hearty, robust flavor. Anyhow, I don't want to write that crap. Nor do I want to tell East Boston women that their skin is falling apart from jet fumes and put Desert Light or whatever it is on their eyelids. And somehow, although I crave designer clothes, I don't know whether I want to wear them to the fourth floor. Oh, God, I want to get out but don't know where to go. [she stopped writing]

The voices in the living room were getting louder. The issue of the nonunion job, it seemed, had been festering for some time. Birdie knew the eruption was bound to come. Sitting in her room and listening to the argument was just as bad as being in the living room and watching it. Birdie would try and get out of the house.

"Where do you think you're going, missy? Marge, isn't she grounded for that God thing?"

"Well, no more, Joe."

"Yes, she is!" Why would her father sidetrack himself from Timmy to pick on her? Timmy was always fair game. What was the big deal picking on her? She was confused until she looked over at Timmy. He seemed pretty self-possessed, considering. Her father's yelling was bouncing off him like hailstones off a brick wall. "Too many uppity kids around here. Got to learn some respect."

For what? Birdie almost said.

"Birdie!" Marge whispered, grasping her own hands. It seemed as if she wanted to touch someone or something else, but was too frightened to move. "Birdie, dear, will you fix Rhonda some Spaghetti-Os? Uh, don't worry, dear. Everything will work out."

"Sure, Mom." Birdie dutifully went to the kitchen and opened the can of Spaghetti-Os. Rhonda had already moved from the living room to the kitchen and was watching Mr. Rogers on the black-and-white set. Joe was getting louder in the other room and Timmy had started to shout.

"Look, I'm telling you, Timmy," Joe roared. "You think me and the guys could get anywhere with that Jew Goldman without a union? Brother, I'd still be at a dollar twenty-five an hour.''

"Rhonda," Birdie said almost desperately, "can't you find anything louder than Mr. Rogers?" Mr. Rogers was calmly talking about feelings people have inside of themselves. "Let me look," Birdie said suddenly, and began to turn the channel dial. She had made one complete circle of clicks and was halfway through another searching for the noisy din of a cartoon when she heard the soft explosion and the thud.

"Joe!" screamed Marge. When Birdie came out of the kitchen Timmy was just getting up off the floor. His bottom lip was torn. The corner seemed to hang loose. Blood poured out. He spat something out into his hand. He spat again. Birdie saw a tooth come out. Joe appeared stunned.

"It's all right, it's all right." Timmy's words were slurred. He glanced at both his parents as if trying to assure them he was okay. But there was an undercurrent of something else. Everyone in the room, including Rhonda now, was trying to reassure themselves about what had happened. Even Timmy's words didn't seem to mean what they were supposed to mean.

"I—" Joe began. "I didn't mean to hit you so hard, Tim. Uh . . . I'm sorry."

"It's all right. It's all right."

Rhonda looked frightened. Birdie leaned down to her ear. "Why don't you go watch Mr. Rogers?"

"I can't," she whispered back. "It's over."

"He didn't mean to hit you that hard," Marge said. Her face was taut and her eyes filled with tears.

"It's all right."

"Here, let me get you a towel," she said.

"I'll go with you to the clinic." Birdie reached for her pocketbook, which was on the couch.

"Yeah, Tim, I think you should go see a doctor." Joe was staring at the blood on his fist. "Look, I'm sorry."

"It's all right. I'll go on my own. It's all right. I'll just get some things from my room."

Nobody dared say anything. It was all very simple, Birdie would think later that day. Timmy went into his room and about four minutes later came out again carrying a small duffel bag. Marge had made up an ice compress. She handed it to him and then he was gone.

CHAPTER 18

"You can't come with me, Birdie!" She had been waiting for him when he came out of the clinic.

"What do you expect me to do? Sleep in Filene's basement?"

"He didn't beat you up. It was me."

"I know, but do you think I want to hang around there?" Timmy didn't answer. "How many stitches did you get, anyway?"

"Seven."

"Did you tell them how it happened?"

"No. Just said I hit it on something."

"Like a father!"

"Look, Birdie, I don't know what you can do, but you can't come with me."

"Well, where are you going? To the tug?"

"Yeah. I think they'll let me sleep on board. I've been thinking about it for a while now."

"You have?" Birdie didn't know why she was surprised, but she was. "Can you sleep on it in the winter?"

"If I have to. They have an oil-burning stove for heat."

"Oh."

"Look, Birdie, I've got my life to lead. You've got yours and that's the way it is. No offense."

"No offense," she said quietly. "Well, will I ever see you again?"

"Of course. I'm not leaving the country, you know. You can always come down to the tug. The Petersens like you. They said so."

"Do you think they'd give me a job?" Birdie said suddenly.

"Birdie, no! Look, I don't mean to hurt your feelings or anything. I know you're the one who's always stood by me. But I don't want them to give you a job. Birdie, can't you understand? You've got to let me have this for myself, for me, just me."

She understood. She understood everything Timmy was saying all too clearly. But what's for me? she kept thinking as she watched him turn toward the waterfront. What in the world is for me? She looked up. She was standing in front of the police station. Barely three months ago she had stood there

143

with what she could only call a terminal case of embarrassment as Timmy and her mother had lain sprawled at the bottom of the steps. Some things undeniably had changed for the better. But she undeniably felt worse. Timmy had hit rock bottom, granite bottom, concrete bottom—whatever those darn steps were made of. Now she was there, metaphorically speaking. (Was this the metaphor she'd been searching for? She hoped not.) But metaphorically or otherwise, she had hit bottom, the pits. Three months ago she'd been full of enthusiasm—"pluck" was her mother's word—about her new job. So she had a messed-up family! She had never really considered herself part of it, anyway. She had been "upwardly mobile," she thought, as she remembered her dreams of the clear, vertical shot that would catapult her from the basement to the fourth floor, from East Boston to Boston, in one smooth arc, like a rainbow curving over the harbor. And now what had happened? She was standing at the bottom of the station steps envious of Timmy. Birdie had never felt more miserable, more impoverished, more dreamless.

"What are you standing here for, looking so glum?"

"Mrs. Pearlowitz!"

"Yes, what's wrong with you? You look like you lost everything." The woman shifted her packages and Birdie saw the tiny marks, the sickening numbered embroidery on her forearm. "How's your brother?"

"Good. Got a new job, holding down two now. He's really"—Birdie paused, searching for a word—"improved."

"No place to go but up," the woman said.

144

"Yeah. I guess you could say that." Birdie had started to walk alongside the woman. "Here, I'll carry your bags. You heading home?"

"Yes. Okay. That's nice of you." Birdie took the bags. The numbers brushed her own arm. "So what's with you? Why do you look so bad?" Birdie was dismayed, not so much by the woman's directness, but by the fact that she must really be looking as rotten as she felt.

"I don't look good, huh?"

"Not so good."

"I'm just feeling, sort of . . . I don't know. I can't explain. . . ." How could she say "trapped" to a woman who had been a nameless, numbered inmate? Mrs. Pearlowitz didn't press her. They were at the door of her building. It was a wooden triple-decker. "I read this thing once," Birdie began suddenly. "It was about the camps." Birdie was speaking rapidly. "It was this boy and in the camps the SS had made him put the noose over his father's head." Her throat went dry.

"Yes?" The woman's voice was taut and husky.

Birdie clamped her eyes shut and shook her head. "I don't know why I'm telling you this. I really don't know why. I'm sorry."

"Don't be. I'll finish the story for you. He put the noose over his father's head. The father begged him to, right?"

"Yes, but there was no choice."

"Oh, no!" Mrs. Pearlowitz raised her finger instructively. "You are wrong. There was always a choice and each choice

145

made us less human. To live was to become not human."
She whispered the last words. Then she took her bags. "Thank
you," she said and went inside.

Birdie looked up and wondered from which window the
screams came in the lost part of a long night.

CHAPTER 19

Cinderella dreamed of getting away from the wicked step-sisters. She chose to be good to the mice. Well, what other choice did she have? The fairy godmother was pure luck, Birdie thought as she watched the movie screen. She took a sip of the large Tab she was sharing with Rhonda and reached into the box of popcorn. As they sewed Cinderella's gown, the mice and birds sang cheerily about women doing the more mundane tasks while the men had the fun of trimming the dress. It was definitely one of Disney's more sexist moments, but Birdie loved the scene. There was something so charming about the way the birds flew in and around the dress with the streamers of ribbons and swagging, while the mice, in their adorable industry, stitched and cut and pinned. It was the ultimate confection—the easy fit, the seamless dress, the whistle-while-you-work, nobody's a jerk. There were talking animals and fairy godmothers spouting bippety-boppety-boo and setting the world to rights.

This was Birdie's cultural event of the week and she was getting more and more depressed. She just prayed that she would have the willpower to stick to Tab and popcorn, but a Three Musketeers bar rattled its gooey swords in the back of her brain, and a Mounds bar was lurking somewhere back there, too. Ooooh, those commercials! She remembered them from her own television days, the little dwarf-cooks pouring on the smooth cascades of chocolate over the almond-coconut filling. Birdie silently marveled at that combination of chocolate, almonds and coconut. Whoever thought it up must have been an incredible genius. It was an inspired mixture, an inspired moment in candy-making history. It was probably the candy equivalent of $E = mc^2$. Her mind was definitely going. Her major mental activity was high-caloric thoughts in animation. On their way home from the movies, as they walked through Maverick Square, Birdie saw Timmy turn in to the sub shop behind the Petersens. She didn't say anything to Rhonda. It was getting late and they had to get home.

I don't want a prince [Birdie wrote that evening in her diary]. *I don't even want clothes, anymore—by mice or Calvin Klein. And there are no fairy godmothers.*

There was the stomp of heavy feet running up the stairs in the building. Cripes, what is it now? Birdie thought. She heard voices in the hallway. It was Richie. And now he was pounding on their door. "Wait a minute, for Chrissakes! Just a minute." But he didn't wait. The door flew open. He stood there, enraged, in his powder-blue leisure suit. A corkscrew of oiled hair fell over his brow. He held the Carol Beth sample kit in his hands. It was smashed and had dirty grease marks all over it.

"You see this, Birdie?" She nodded numbly. Behind him stood Lainie. Her cheek was purple and swollen, her right eye a puffed slit. "I drove over it in my car. Don't never go sneaking around helping Lainie again. Helping her become some goddam businesswoman. They're all lesbians anyhow." He flung the kit across the room. Fragments of bottles, tubes and tiny pots scattered over the floor. "I swear to God, Birdie, you do that again and I'll kill ya!"

"No, you won't!" The voice trembled not with fear but conviction. The voice was so different that Birdie was not sure from whom it came. But it was Marge and she was four feet behind Richie holding a glass. "Get out of the way, Birdie. This isn't iced tea."

The rage drained out of Richie and he suddenly looked pale. "What is it?"

"Lye—and it's going right in your face if you make one move. I'm sick of men beating up on people around here. I've called the police and they're coming and you're not moving till they get here." Then, as if on cue, a door buzzer rang downstairs. "Lainie, you get it. They have the wrong apartment," Marge said.

"Lainie! Lainie, honey!" Richie cried.

But she didn't look at him. She just looked down at the

mashed tubes and chunks and spills of color on the carpet.

Richie took a quick look at Marge, turned and dashed out of the room. The three women stood silent and unmoving until they heard the front door slam downstairs.

"Let me get this stuff back in the bottle." Marge turned slowly around and began walking cautiously toward the kitchen.

"You should have put on rubber gloves, Ma," Lainie said.

"Rubber gloves! Lainie, he could have killed you by then."

"Well, don't spill it on your hands."

"I won't," said Marge as her daughters followed her down the hall. "I was more worried about the wall-to-wall."

After the lye had been restored to the bottle, Marge, Lainie and Birdie collapsed around the kitchen table. Marge cupped her chin in her hand and stared down at the table. She fiddled with the spoon in the sugar bowl. "My first act of violence."

"It wasn't violent, Ma," Lainie said. "You didn't throw it."

"Yeah, Ma, so don't start thinking about confession."

"Who said anything about confession? And what makes you think if I had thrown it I would feel guilty?"

Birdie thought that if her mother had chirped bippety-boppety-boo and turned a pumpkin into a coach she could have not been more surprised. Indeed, she had been completely amazed ever since her mother had walked into the room with the glass of lye.

"What are you looking so startled for—the both of you?" Marge said, opening her eyes wide at her daughters as if to mimic them. "I'd do it all over again. I was defending my children, my daughters!" She mumbled something under her breath.

"What?" Birdie and Lainie both said at the same time.

Marge closed her eyes, smiled and rubbed her forehead. "Oh," she laughed softly, "I just said, 'Violence and motherhood.' "

"What are you talking about?" Lainie asked.

"It's suppose to be motherhood and apple pie," Birdie said. "Mom," she asked suddenly, "did Dad ever hit you?"

Marge looked up. Her pale brown eyes reflected nothing. She said nothing and Birdie wished she had never asked the question.

"Lainie," Marge said, turning to her older daughter, "when was the last time you had apple pie?"

"Yesterday at a 'participating McDonald's,' as Rhonda calls them. Doesn't even look like pie. It's not wedge-shaped, you know. It comes in a cardboard tube." The three started laughing.

"And do I look like an apple-pie mom?" Marge chuckled.

"Not with those dead rabbits on your feet!" Birdie pointed at Marge's slippers.

At this they all roared. Marge doubled over. She was laughing so hard she could hardly speak. "You mean . . . you mean . . . ." She began the sentence about three times before she could get it out. "You mean that Florence Hendersen or Mrs. Brady doesn't wear slippers like these on 'The Brady Bunch'?"

"Hell, no!" Lainie gasped, wiping tears from her eyes. "Mr. Brady would divorce her!"

"They'd de-Bunch her!" shrieked Birdie. "But don't worry, you could wear them on 'The Flintstones.'"

"I've got to. I've got bunions!" Marge gasped with laughter.

"Oh, Ma Walton has bunions!"

"Not Paris Wells!" Birdie offered.

"Never!" said Marge. "Oh, Lord, aren't we the all-American family."

Marge got up from the table, wiping the tears from her eyes. "It's so dark in here," she said, as if noticing for the first time in twenty years. "Birdie, raise those shades and get me a glass of iced tea. There's a pitcher in the refrigerator."

CHAPTER

Birdie didn't tell the Saccharellis the part about when her mother said she was sick of men beating up on everybody, because she really didn't want them to know what she suspected about her father. Let them think Richie was the only one. But she did tell them about the smashed kit and the lye and the police.

"All Lainie needs to do is go get herself a court order forbidding that jerk to visit her, either at her place or your parents'. And if he violates it, they'll put him in the slammer faster than he knows what's happening." Vinnie paused, crossed his arms and tilted his head toward the ceiling. "Man, oh, man! I never knew your mother had it in her. Some gutsy lady!"

"Yeah," Birdie said.

"What's wrong, Birdie?" Rose Saccharelli asked. "You sound funny. You didn't think it was right, what your mom did?"

"Oh, no. It was fine. Definitely the right thing to do. The only thing. No choice." Birdie felt a queasiness high in her chest, almost to her throat. But she wasn't really worried about vomiting. She was worried about crying. It was as if a huge teardrop had been welling up inside of her for days and now it was ready to spill. "I—I—" She lifted her hand to her brow so that it was partly covering her eyes. "I do feel funny." The tear began to squeeze out. She instantly made herself one promise. She would not blame anything about the way she felt on Timmy or Lainie or even her mother now.

"What is it, Birdie?" Rose Saccharelli had her arm around Birdie's shoulders.

"It sounds crazy, I know." Birdie was crying softly. "I feel left behind with no place to go . . . I just don't know where to go!"

"What do you mean?" Gloria asked. "Who left you behind?"

"I don't know. Nobody, really. I just feel that way. And Gloria, don't be mad, but I really want to quit Filene's. I just don't like it and I don't know where I'm going there."

"The fourth floor, of course!" Gloria said. "And then, you know, the merchandising training program, then the buyer—" But Rose motioned Gloria to stop.

"That may be where you're going, Gloria, but not me," said Birdie. "I mean, I really feel disloyal saying this."

"Nonsense!" Rose and Vinnie both spoke the word at the

154

same time. Then Rose continued. "Look, it isn't disloyal not to like the same things Gloria does, even though you're best friends. But, Birdie, you can't quit now. You agreed to stay until school starts, right?"

"Yeah."

"Well, that's only two weeks," Rose said. "It's not going to look good on your resumé if you quit now. You can stand it for two more weeks."

"I guess so." It was amazing how much better she felt already, just being able to talk with someone about this. Maybe you could stand anything if you had someone to talk to. "But then what?"

"Well, now that's a good question. It's not just the job, huh?"

"I don't like the job and . . . ."

"But you want to like something?" Rose Saccharelli seemed almost psychic to Birdie.

"Yeah. I mean, you know, Gloria and I, well, you know, we want to get out of East Boston, and now Gloria has a way."

"But it's not right for you."

"Yeah."

"Well, there's more than one way to skin a cat, Birdie," Rose said matter-of-factly. For the first time in weeks, Birdie felt something akin to hope, real hope. It was as if Rose Saccharelli had pierced a tiny hole in the blanket of depression that had swallowed Birdie, and now a pinprick of light and air was coming through. "First of all, Birdie, you have to do something you like, that you want to do, or you'll never really be able to 'get out,' as you put it."

"I don't mean to sound preachy," Vinnie began. "But,

Birdie, you've got to know what you're going *to*, not just *from*."

"It does sound preachy, Vinnie. But it is the truth. Where do you want to go?"

"The other side."

"Yeah, but, Birdie"—Vinnie was looking directly at her—"can we narrow it down a bit? There's a lot of choices over there." There was that word again.

"I don't know. That's my problem."

"Well, now," Vinnie spoke slowly, "it seems obvious that you've already made one choice."

"What's that?"

"Not to work at Filene's. We should say that this seems not to be your chosen field. Gloria, get me a beer, would you?"

"Yeah, that's right. Filene's is not my chosen field."

"The question is: What might be your chosen field?" Everyone was listening intently to Vinnie, but Birdie was not at all sure where he was heading. "If I may be so bold, it seems to me that there is one obvious area in which you are above average."

"Oh, Vinnie!" Rose said with disdain. "How sweet of you. You sure do have a way with words."

"I don't!" Vinnie nearly shouted. "But Birdie does! Not only above average, but superior. Believe me, Birdie is going to have as much a part in your getting to Houston as anyone."

"He's right," Rose said with delight. "I wouldn't be past chapter two without you."

"Well," Vinnie continued, "the answer's simple."

"Of course!" Rose exclaimed. "You're Margaret! You're a natural writer and editor."

"What are you two talking about? I don't want to write a romance novel."

"Not a romance novel, you nut! A newspaper!" Vinnie boomed. "You get a job with the *Globe*. You go into that journalism internship program they run for high school seniors."

"I'm not sure," she said slowly.

"It's your choice, Birdie."

CHAPTER 21

So [wrote Birdie in her diary], Deadline for Love *might come true, or should I say be realized in ways we never thought, nor Mrs. Saccharelli's dangling participles ever suggested. I don't have to get pregnant or go to work on a competing newspaper first. I just have to submit two samples of my writing, fill out a questionnaire and have an interview. Big deal. It is. I've got all these pieces that were published in the school paper and I hate every one of them now. They all seem so immature and over-written, especially the one about graffiti on the restroom walls. Yuck! I can't believe I wrote it. One or two are possibilities, but I really think I'll have to write something new, and what could that be?*

Writing in her diary was not really helping her hatch any brilliant ideas for an essay. So she closed the notebook and rested her elbows on the sill of the open window. Although her bedroom faced the front of the house, she had always thought of her window as a back view. The view was not of the harbor, but of Webster Street, the small park it bordered, the other houses surrounding the park and then just beyond them, the airport. It seemed a confined, enclosed scene, whereas the water view never seemed that way to her. On this warm and placid Sunday morning, however, she cupped her chin in her hands and watched. The church bells were ringing and Birdie guessed that Benny Arlette had just gotten his jollies from doing whatever he did with the holy water and that Timmy was getting ready to do whatever it was he did after Mass with his unholy water and mops. The trees in the park that the mayor had planted just before his last campaign for reelection had, despite jet fumes, dogs and other tree vandals, survived. Indeed, Birdie observed they were no longer in the clinging-to-life stage, but had advanced and had produced some mildly healthy-looking leaves. Several of the women from houses on the bordering streets of the park had taken time to water them. They were mostly older women who no longer had kids to nurture. Birdie would see them out there at odd hours with their cans and pitchers. Even now, as people walked diagonally across the park to the Church of the Annunciation on the other corner, she would notice an older woman glance occasionally at one of the saplings. These women, she thought—it was as if they couldn't give up fussing with living things, especially very young living things. Birdie looked straight down into the tangled front yard. She couldn't see the chipped nose from this angle, just the folds of her robes. From this altitude, the madonna was definitely less offensive to her. Imagine! Birdie thought, what her mom would do if she could read Birdie's mind. With some fancy footwork, as they said, you could imagine almost any face on that statue, even a man's, even Phyllis Dougherty's!

Birdie got up, walked back to her desk, took out some paper and began to write.

I want to be liked by men, not worshipped. Respected, not cherished. There is a madonna with a chipped nose in our front yard, and too many people think . . . .

It was an eight-hundred-word essay on people's expectations and illusions about women, and the differences between deities and role models. Except for the Virgin Mary and Paris Wells, the names were changed to protect the innocent. But she wrote about Gloria Saccharelli and Rose, and herself and Marge Flynn and Lainie and Phyllis Dougherty and the women who watered the mayor's trees. And she wrote about her father and Richie and Benny Arlette and Father Leo and that line of six boys waiting their turn. It was an essay about disappointment and hope, about dreams of perfection and feelings of destruction. And she wrote about how this was true not just for East Boston or Catholics, but for every town and everyone. If they didn't have a chipped madonna, they would find one—metaphorically speaking, that is.

CHAPTER
22

Birdie walked up Sumner Street. It was freezing cold and a few flakes of snow had started to fall. Christmas decorations had been up for at least a week in Maverick Square, and now the people were starting to light up their houses. The single, electric orange candle in the window was a popular decoration. Some people had plastic Santa Clauses and Frosty the Snowmen on their doors. There was one house that Birdie was especially anxious to reach to see if they had drawn their parlor curtains open yet this year to show their own Christmas creation. The house was halfway up Sumner Street in a particular stretch that had no front yards, because the houses were built flush to the sidewalk. A passerby could look directly into the front room. The curtains had been drawn, and, in spite of the bitter cold, Birdie stopped to observe the scene within. A Ping-Pong table had been pulled up to the large window and was covered with fake snow. An electric train chugged merrily along an oval track. Santa Claus sat on top of the engine. In the center of the oval was a crèche. Little plastic sheep and cows stood around. At one end of the oval was a model of the White House; at the other end was one of the State House, gold dome and all. Were they in some way hedging their bets? When she got home she would get Rhonda and bundle her up to come and see it. She had been wondering all week if there might be a story in this for the interns' column in the *Globe* that came out twice a month. She wasn't sure what it was— Christmas decor in East Boston? Church and State? The chances of the *Globe*'s actually publishing a second piece of hers were almost nil. But her chipped madonna piece had been printed because a woman editor on the review committee for the program had found it to be "extraordinary," and Birdie had been encouraged to keep writing. She doubted, though, that they'd want another piece with religious statuary.

Birdie walked on quickly up the street. As she turned into her own walkway she noticed that her mother had strewn the lights in the bushes near the madonna and you could really see her nose now. "Here's lookin' at you, kid!" Birdie said and skipped up the stairs.

"What are you so bright eyed and bushy tailed about?" Lainie asked.

"She's always that way when she comes home from the *Globe*," Joe said. "Maybe she's drinking on the job. Newspaper people are famous for their drinking."

"Oh, God, no! Is that true, Birdie?" Marge came out of the kitchen.

"Mother!"

"Well, how do I know what's going on down there?"

Down there! Birdie thought. Her mother spoke of the *Globe* as if it were the Arctic Circle.

"Well, after what they wrote about your brother and that prank last summer, I just can't see how they'd hire his sister."

At first Birdie was simply stupefied, but then she felt angry. "You know what's wrong with you people?" Birdie's voice was intense.

"No, Birdie, tell us." Joe folded his paper and looked belligerently at his daughter.

"Okay." She was trying hard to control her voice. She wanted this to connect. She wanted to shake them up and she did not want it all to culminate in her being called missy. "I'll tell you, both of you, Mom and yourself. You aren't used to your children succeeding. This whole darn family is so programmed for failure, you don't know what achievement is."

"I know what sass is!" Marge began.

"Now just hold on and, for God's sake, don't call me missy! Look, here's Lainie an area manager now, as of last week. And what do you say to her when she gets it? 'Good, but don't keep bothering Birdie to do your bookkeeping.' "

"Yeah!" said Lainie, suddenly ruffled. "I've been figuring the commissions myself since August."

"Well," Marge said, "I'm very sorry, Lainie. I just didn't know."

"It's not that you didn't know, Ma! It's that you didn't expect it." Birdie paused. "Couldn't imagine it. It was the same with Timmy. First time you see him in two months and he's carrying those books and you say what for and he tells you—all that stuff about minimum papers for skippering. And you say he'll never make it! Right to his face you say that." Joe kept reading his paper. He was listening but did not look up. "Well," Birdie continued, "I've got news for you. He is going to make it. He can read everything he needs to know for the test now." Nobody had called her missy yet. Things seemed different, somehow. Birdie then said something she had never imagined herself saying. "Ma, you believe in *her*."

"Who?" asked Marge.

"The madonna in our front yard." Marge nodded silently, warily, as if she didn't know what might come next. "Well," Birdie continued, "believe in us."

Marge inhaled sharply. She put her hand on her chest lightly, almost as though she were trying to touch her own heart. "Birdie! Birdie! I don't know what to make of this! I love you. All of you! So much!" And Birdie knew that she meant it.

"Loving is believing, too, Ma."

"Birdie"—her father spoke, breaking his silence—"what you're saying here is hard."

"I know it's hard."

"Birdie"—her father scratched his head—"we do believe in you, but . . . but are you trying to say"—he groped for a word—"I mean . . . you're better than us?"

Birdie wasn't sure whether it was a question or a statement. Was he angry or pleased? She searched his face, looking for some clue. She found no clues. But there was something there that startled her. Her father was looking at her, really looking at her for the first time ever. He was looking right into her eyes. He shook his head as if to clear it, coughed and went back to his paper. Birdie coughed, too. She hoped that it would bring him back from behind the paper. "Dad?"

He peeked over the top. "Yeah?"

"You think that I think that we're better than you and Ma? Is that what you're trying to say?"

"Naw. Forget it."

"Don't forget it," Marge said suddenly.

"I mean—Ma, Dad," Birdie spoke slowly. "It's not a question of better."

"Maybe you're right," Joe said without anger. He folded his paper and looked at them both.

It was a strange experience, a strange conversation. Nobody exactly knew the other person's meaning, but nobody was getting mad, either. It wasn't as if they were just trying to listen to each other. It was as if they were trying to hear for the first time ever.

CHAPTER 23

Birdie had Rhonda bundled up in her arms. She was some bundle. Underneath her snowsuit she had on her pajamas, the kind with feet, and then Marge had brought out a small puffy cover to wrap her in. Now Birdie was jogging down Sumner Street. She had felt so funny after the conversation with her parents that she had asked if she could take Rhonda to see the window with the train. It had indeed been a real conversation and not a fight.

"Wait'll you see this, Rhonda. It's much better than that thing you were watching on television."

"It wasn't a thing. It was the Smurfs' Christmas special."

"Well, this is better."

"Maybe there'll be Smurfs in it."

"Possibly. You cold?"

"Nope."

The snow was coming down more thickly now and several flakes landed on Birdie's eyelashes. She felt Rhonda's warm breath on her cheek.

"Here we are." She hoisted Rhonda higher on her shoulder.

"Aaaah! It's beautiful. Look at the train and the Santa and those angels!"

"Where?" Birdie hadn't noticed the angels.

"Right there by that gold top on that building."

"Look at the shepherds." Birdie pointed. A gust of snow swirled right up into their faces, which were pressed close to each other.

When Birdie looked up, Rhonda, speaking softly onto her cheek, said, "I don't think they're shepherds. I think they're cowboys from the Fisher Price Frontier Town."

"Oh," said Birdie.

"The cows are from the Hasbro Walk-Around Farm. Just like the one Grandma got me."

"No assembly required?" Birdie said.

"Yeah. That's the one."

They watched a little bit longer and, in spite of the cold, felt cozy wrapped up together within the snowy, starless night.

They passed a small alley on their way home, where there was a gap in the buildings right down to the waterfront. For a moment they stopped to look at the harbor. The snowy gale winds had transformed it into a white, swirling world without

167

boundaries. But out of the white veil the red and green lights of a tug appeared softly. "Look!" whispered Rhonda. "It looks like a floating Christmas tree!"

"It does."

"I hope Timmy's on it. It must feel beautiful to ride a floating Christmas tree through the night."

This is a tugboat story of sorts that is not entirely suitable for children. So we will not call it "Little Toot." It is about a boy, a young man almost, whose life had become a prank. He had flunked everything. Three F's and a D. He'd even flunked sex. He couldn't do it when he was supposed to, when his turn came with the girl in the car. And then he went with some of his friends one night to a synagogue and he did the only thing he and his friends knew how to do—desecrate. And for one minute, or maybe it was just twenty seconds, he felt great. He told me that himself. He felt power. And he felt good and ugly and big and bad all at once. Oh, he was plenty sorry afterward. He hadn't meant it. He told them that at the hearing. It was a prank. That's what everyone had called it, even the judge.

He was put on probation and worked hard to pay the fine. But he began to realize something odd, which was that what he had done was not a prank but real, and that what he had become as a person was not real but a prank. It was always easier to try for failure than success, because there were fewer risks that way and no responsibility. It's not a great way to live but it's tolerable for a while, at least until you begin to realize that you're not real and that being dead might be preferable to being unreal with a practical joke of a life.

One day he was standing on a pier in East Boston and a tugboat had an engine failure. It was heading directly toward the pier where he stood. One failure heading toward another. That was what he was thinking. The woman on the deck started shouting and signaling for him to catch a rope she was about to throw. He didn't want to catch it. He didn't want to even try for it. You know why—all the same old reasons.

The boy stood frozen on the end of the pier. Time seemed to stop for him, and for this one moment all chances were to be taken. Life and meaning had telescoped. He leaped into the air, straight up, and met the rope that sailed out of the sky, grabbed it and slapped it on a post in time. This solitary act had become both his first and last chance to do something right.

The rest of his story is not one of chance or doing right but becoming real. He signed onto the tug as a deckhand. He couldn't read beyond fourth-grade level, but he taught himself navigation. After two years of helping every kind of ship imaginable into Boston harbor he began to think about the sea. Through his boss's recommendation he received his seaman's certificate and now serves on one of the big ocean-going tugs. His goal is to become eligible to take the third mate exam. This is the first step toward chief mate and, ultimately, his master's ticket. He has become an excellent navigator. The kid who could barely read has the book learning part "down pat." He just has to get the hours now which means most likely that Timothy Flynn, whose life until recently was a prank, will eventually be certified as a master for "any vessel, any tonnage, any ocean."

Joe Flynn set the paper down and looked up at his daughter. "You wrote this?"

"Sure. Who else?" She looked up from one of her college text books and shrugged.

"You're no slouch, Bird!"

Poetic he was not, Birdie thought, but he'd come a long way, her dad. "No slouch" was okay, but "any ocean" was definitely preferable—metaphorically speaking.

Want someone who'll ask tough questions that'll force you to think? Read

ROBERT CORMIER

D. H. Conley School Library

Selected from

WITHDRAWN
THE
GODFATHER

Mario Puzo

Supplementary material by the staff of Literacy Volunteers of New York City

WRITERS' VOICES

SIGNAL HILL

ATTENTION READERS: We would like to hear what
you think about our books. Please send your comments
or suggestions to:

Signal Hill Publications
P.O. Box 131
Syracuse, NY 13210-0131

•   •   •

SIGNAL HILL

Additional material
© 1991 Signal Hill Publications
A publishing imprint of Laubach Literacy International

Printed in the United States of America

97 96 95 94 10 9 8 7 6 5 4 3 2

First printing: March 1991

ISBN 0-929631-22-6

The words 'Writers' Voices' are a trademark of
Signal Hill Publications.

Cover designed by Paul Davis Studio
Interior designed by Caron Harris

Signal Hill is a not-for-profit publisher. The proceeds
from the sale of this book support the national and
international programs of Laubach Literacy International.

PRINTED WITH
SOY INK™

This book was printed on 100% recycled paper
which contains 50% post-consumer waste.

Acknowledgments

We gratefully acknowledge the generous support of the following foundations and corporations that made the publication of WRITERS' VOICES and NEW WRITERS' VOICES possible: An anonymous foundation; The Vincent Astor Foundation; Booth Ferris Foundation; Exxon Corporation; James Money Management, Inc.; Knight Foundation; Philip Morris Companies Inc.; Scripps Howard Foundation; The House of Seagram; and H.W. Wilson Foundation.

This book could not have been realized without the kind and generous cooperation of the author, Mario Puzo, his publisher, G.P. Putnam's Sons, and his agent, Candida Donadio of Donadio and Ashworth, Inc.

We deeply appreciate the contributions of the following suppliers: Cam Steel Die Rule Works Inc. (steel cutting die for display); Canadian Pacific Forest Products Ltd. (text stock); ComCom (text typesetting); Horizon Paper Co., Inc. and Domtar Fine Papers (cover stock); MCUSA (display header); Delta Corrugated Container (corrugated display); Phototype Color Graphics (cover color separations); and Arcata Graphics Company/Buffalo (cover and text printing and binding).

Our thanks to Paul Davis Studio and Myrna Davis, Paul Davis, Jeanine Esposito, Alex Ginns and Frank Begrowicz for their inspired design of the covers of these books. Thanks also to Caron Harris for her sensitive design of the interior of this book, Karen Bernath for design of maps and diagrams, and Ron Bel Bruno for his timely help.